# VAMPIRES OF ATLANTIS

# VAMPIRES OF ATLANTIS

## A LOVE STORY

## BRIAN STABLEFORD

**WILDSIDE PRESS**

*For Blackie.*

Published by Wildside Press LLC.
www.wildsidebooks.com

# I

The events of the story I'm about to tell you happened a long time ago, before the turn of the century.

It was after graduation, when I walked away from university with my lower second in sociology. I didn't deserve anything better, although I wasn't the only one who reckoned I was clever. I'd done a lot of reading during my time there, but not very much of it had been relevant to the course and almost none of it figured on the official reading list. When I first got there, the best part of two hundred miles away from home, uni felt more like a holiday camp, after the discipline of school, than a place of work, and I'd treated it as such. I'd trusted in my innate fluency to write the requisite number of essays and get me through the exams without overmuch application and revision, and it had worked, after a fashion.

Some might say that I'd underperformed—some of those entitled to express an opinion did, in fact—but I'd achieved the prime objective of getting through three years of pleasant company without being thrown out, and coming out of it with a bit of paper that said I was a Bachelor of Arts. I didn't think it was lying; I was, after all, still a bachelor, having been dumped a few weeks before finals—timing that probably hadn't done much for my final result, although I'm not about to put the blame on it, if any blame needs to be attached—by the girl I'd been going out with most of the three-year stint, whose name was Alison, and I thought of myself as having an artistic temperament, even though I couldn't draw very well, couldn't play a musical instrument and had never managed to finish any of the novels I'd optimistically started writing.

I still haven't finished any, even after all these years. Maybe a change of genre is what I needed all along, although back in those days, I was very sniffy about autobiography. "As Winston Churchill said," I used to say, "there are lies, damn lies, statistics, history and autobiography." There was usually some smartarse around who would point out that Winnie, as my late grandfather used to call him, had stopped at statistics, which set up the punch-line of the joke. "That's what history says," I would announce then, "but that's because historians censored the rest to shield their wounded vanity."

Although it was a joke, it was pretty much what I believed. I was always skeptical about anything anybody tried to tell me, especially if they swore that it was the truth. I almost cheered in one of the few lectures I bothered to attend on the methodology course, when one of the lecturers—some bearded pillock in a corduroy jacket whose name I can't recall—made the same point, in less Wildean terms, by saying that nobody ever wrote autobiography in order to tell the truth, but only to justify themselves, to get themselves off the hook, and that in order to do that, they would lie through their teeth from Tuesday to doomsday.

I think it was the same guy who advised us all, in his work-weary fashion, always to employ "the Claud Cockburn principle" in approaching any supposed item of non-fiction, the Claud Cockburn principle being that you always start out any serious enquiry by asking yourself: "Why is this lying bastard lying to me?" on the assumption that he almost always is, whether he's a journalist, a politician, an estate agent, a banker, a sociologist, a historian, a physicist or the pope. And the basic reason is almost always because he's trying to justify himself, to get himself off the hook.

I suppose I ought to begin by assuring you that this story is different, but I can't and I won't, because you should always apply the Claud Cockburn principle to yourself, as well as everyone else. We lie to ourselves even more than we lie to other people, even more insistently, and for exactly the same reasons.

As I say, all this happened a long time ago. How can I possibly trust my memory? And how can I possibly trust myself, even if I could remember correctly, to repeat what my memory tells me without tweaking it. We alter memories every time we recall them, and although transforming them is a slow and painful business—because they resist, and how!—we can generally force them, given time enough, to undergo a measure of metamorphosis, usually in the interests of making ourselves look a shade less shitty and pathetic than we really are.

Has there been time enough for my memory to have scarred over the wounds it suffered back then? I don't think so, and I don't think that writing it down, even if it adds a further inevitable layer of distortion, is going to achieve that semi-healing either, but that's not the objective. If anything, I suppose reliving the sequence of events in prose is more likely to open the wounds and start them bleeding again, but that's not the objective either. Consciously, at least, the objective is to try to make more sense of it than I was able to make at the time. Unconsciously— well, how the hell would I know? You can decide, if you bother to read all the way to the end, and if you find that I've managed to get that far, for once in my life.

Anyway, if I were to say that this is exactly how it happened, and that all the dialogue is reported, word for word, the way it was actually spoken, I wouldn't be able to blame you for taking it with a pinch of salt. I can't be sure myself of the dialogue, or some of the incidental detail. In fact, the only things I am absolutely certain about are the vampires of Atlantis—who were probably never real to start with, and thus stood in no need of subtle falsification—and the love. The love was real; if it weren't, there'd be no point in writing its story, because, let's be honest, there hasn't been anything else in my life that would justify an essay in autobiography.

Alison, for instance, was never a story worth telling, even though we were together for more than two years, and even though there was a bit of love in there somewhere, on both sides, and not just sex and huddling together for mutual reassurance, because even a holiday camp can be a little scary when you're a long way from home and out of your element. I could say the same about a couple of other relationships of similar duration and ultimate irrelevance, but all of that is best passed over, if not in silence, at least in derisory summary.

So, to begin again, at the beginning, I left university with my 2.2 and I went home to Leeds.

I did that partly because I had nowhere else to go, having failed to get any of the jobs I'd applied for before graduation, probably because my referees had said, accurately enough, that although I was a bright enough lad, I hadn't yet learned to buckle down to serious work. Also, of course, my degree was in sociology. If I'd had a quid for every time I heard the old joke beginning "What do you say to a sociology graduate?" I wouldn't have had to get a stopgap job at all, but nobody pays you a wage to listen to put-downs. Anyway, it wasn't true by then. Since the minimum wage had come in, three months before graduation, fast food outlets had suddenly become deeply reluctant to hire anyone who qualified for it. By the summer of 1999, it was beginning to look as if the sacred right to be on the wrong end of orders for a Big Mac and fries would be reserved henceforth to seventeen- and eighteen-year-olds and what we were still calling, in those primitive days, "illegal immigrants." Because I was twenty-one and legal, I had no alternative but to raise my sights—toward regions, alas, where the reputation that preceded me proved something of a disincentive to would-be employers.

The other reason that I went back to Leeds instead of staying down south, where it would probably have been easier to find work, was that I had somewhere there to live. My Dad had died during my first year at uni—asbestosis contracted way before the partial 1985 ban—and he'd left the flat he'd bought when he and Mum divorced to Steve, me and

Lily. Steve moved into it for a while before he joined up, and then got a letting agent to rent it out to students at Leeds University until he finished his nine-year stint, or until I or Lily needed it, whichever happened first. In the summer of 1999 Lily was still at school, with a year to go before heading off to uni herself, and Steve was on deployment, so the flat was all mine, at least for a while. Dad's life insurance had paid off the mortgage, so all I'd have to find would be the council tax, the utility bills and the third of the notional rent that went into Lily's "trust fund," to see her through university when she went. Steve had generously said that he no longer needed his share of the rental money we'd been splitting, as his army pay was more than adequate to support in the manner to which he was rapidly becoming accustomed.

The flat was in Harehills Lane, which was only a bus ride away from Mum and the kid sister, as well as giving easy access to the city center, but the advantage I'd appreciated most when I first inherited my share of it was that it had allowed me to tell my friends and acquaintances at the uni that I now owned property in Dorset. It was a waste of irony, of course. None of them, even the southerners who thought that anywhere north of Hertfordshire is untracked wilderness with a few derelict coal mines, ever thought for an instant that I might mean the posh southern county. Only Leeds folk actually knew where the county's humbler namesake was—"Oh, yeah," they would say, smugly, "out past St. James's and the Corporation Cemetery"—but even the others had an innate skepticism that simply wouldn't let them believe that I might ever have set foot in Weymouth, let alone Poole. I might have done better simply to tell the smartarses that I'd been to school in Dorset, saving the revelation that I meant Thorn Walk Secondary for a possible punch-line, but that would have been a bit too esoteric even for me.

It wasn't a great flat—Dad had been under a lot of pressure, in more ways than one, when he's bought it, and he hadn't exactly equipped and furnished in the best possible taste, but it was a place to go. It was a safe haven, where I wouldn't have to pay an astronomical rent, and a secure base from which to plan my next move, if and when I figured out what move I wanted to make, and managed to obtain sufficient moral credit to make myself a viable applicant for it. In the meantime, however, I needed a stopgap job, in order to feed myself, pay the bills and save myself the ultimate ignominy of having to move back in with Mum and Lily.

Fortunately, the introduction of the minimum wage had coincided with the initial wildfire spread of call centers, which weren't yet being relocated *en masse* to Mumbai and the Philippines. That allowed me to cash in on the only asset I had, apart from my sociology degree. Although I'd been born and bred just off Easterly Road and had never had an elocution lesson in my life, my accent wasn't nearly as thick as it might have been. I'd learned to suppress it even further while I was doing my three years at the uni; even at Leeds University, the only way for a Leeds lad to fit in would have been to ape the manners and mores of the southern majority, so you can imagine what it's like down in the actual south.

Ten years later, the theory got round that UK customers actually feel more comfortable talking to someone with a Northern accent, because it reassures them that they aren't talking to Mumbai, but in 1999, a more neutral manner of speaking was reckoned an asset. The people running the call center weren't, of course, allowed to say that one of the qualifications for the job was a posher voice than most people who'd go for that kind of a job possessed. Their ads only specified a "good telephone manner"—but I could do politeness and patience too, even though I wasn't female.

Ninety per cent of the front-liners back then were lasses, perhaps because a "good telephone manner" is one of those things that most females develop naturally in their teenage years, like bulimia, PMT and deodorant addiction. Lads didn't usually develop a "good telephone manner" back in the twentieth century because they tended to take an essentially utilitarian view of the phone, making short and functional calls, whereas lasses found a perverse kind of intimacy in the form and touch of a plastic receiver, which delivered gossip as if by magic. Not that I was a common-or-garden male chauvinist, of course, even before I changed—we northern scum don't always conform to stereotype.

Anyway, the generalization is out of date now, because smart phones have changed the game somewhat, but it was true at the time. I think I might even have been the beneficiary of a measure of affirmative action, favoring male applicants in order that the workforce didn't seem to be exclusively female. One way or another, though, I practically walked into a job in one of the first Leeds-based centers, working for a company that even now, after all these years, I'd prefer not to name, in case they take offence at my opinion of their operation. If I were still the kind of person who made up fake Winston Churchill quotes—and I guess I must be—I'd amend the one I just recalled to: "As Winston Churchill said, there are lies, damn lies, statistics, history, autobiography and customer service."

Nowadays, of course, everyone's customer service department gives you lots of buttons to press on your phone, before a recorded message puts you on hold for ten minutes, and then you get "accidentally" cut off, so it often isn't until the fifth or sixth attempt, if you have that much patience, that you actually get through to the professional liar who will promise to sort out your billing problem—and might actually pass the suggestion to on someone who can do that, if your call log shows that this is the fifth or sixth time you've complained—but in the archaic days of the twentieth century, the rigmarole was still much simpler, and you usually got through to the professional liar right away, so we front-liners had to be a lot slicker.

You might not think there's much of an art and skill to that, unless you've actually done the job, but you'd be wrong. For one thing, there was a long list of things that we were absolutely forbidden to say, requiring a certain mastery of circumlocution as well as an unshakable calm politeness even in the face of the worst abuse and distress. For another, we had to master the particular jargon related to the product for whose support we were providing support, and also had to keep that jargon up to date as the product changed its nature and its various faults became gradually manifest.

The second issue probably wasn't very important if you were working for a power company, or even an insurance company, but the job I got was in the communications industry. Anyone with the slightest knowledge of history knows how rapidly that was changing back in 1999, with products being updated practically by the week and bugs becoming manifest almost by the day. All call centers were pretty much alike in those days, but the one on Scott Hall Road where I went to work provided a sterner challenge than most and also seemed a trifle incestuous, by virtue of the fact that we were fielding queries on behalf of a company that made, installed and customized all kinds of telephone equipment, personal and institutional, up to and including call centers.

With regard to the first part of the problem, the art bears an eerie resemblance to pretending to be a robot bound but three hundred laws instead of three, but it *is* an art, of sorts, believe me. The second part of the problem could be even more challenging, especially for the teenagers who made up the bulk of the workforce, and was partly responsible for the fast turnover of the workforce and the willingness of the Management to hire university graduates whom they knew full well were only looking for a stopgap while shopping around for a job with better prospects. Although there was only one other graduate in my intake, and four already on the strength, it was really stopgap work for practically everyone who manned the phones, because people can only take so much of a job that involves dealing sensitively with boorish clients who are confused or angry even before they're put on hold, and twice as bad afterwards. We got calls from customers who were resentful because they were too stupid to follow the instructions telling them how to work their kit, customers who were livid because the kit couldn't do precisely what they wanted it to do, and customers who were incandescent because they thought they'd been overcharged—that was about it.

Although I did a two week basic training course in the kinds of products the company sold, at a training center at company HQ, not at Scott Hall Road itself, the only real advice I was allowed to give was script-based stuff that didn't get much more sophisticated than "Have you checked that the unit's plugged in?" In essence, my job was to fob off fools and troublemakers as best I could and take down details of real problems so that I could refer them to the appropriate technical staff or the accounts department, with profuse assurances that somebody would phone back shortly with real help.

I didn't expect the work to be too difficult, and, once I'd got the hang of it, it wasn't, but it's peculiarly taxing having to maintain a polite front in the face of such relentless incompetence and hostility. Apart from the fact that the money was enough to feed me and pay the bills, the job's main advantage, when I applied for it, seemed to be the "flexibility" of the shift system. That, I figured, would allow me to vary my hours, taking time out to attend interviews for real jobs if and when they came up, and would make overtime easily available if I wanted it. I hadn't quite cottoned on when I read the ad that "flexible" was advertising-speak for "arbitrarily variable."

I didn't intend to be in the job for more than a few months, and I wasn't—but what I didn't expect, when I started it, was that it would be a watershed in my life, and that I wouldn't be the same person when I came out of it, after less than a year, as I had been when I went into it. Three years of university, even in the alien world of "down south" hadn't really made much of a dent in my character, but a few months in the bizarre alternative universe of a nondescript building in Scott Hall Road transformed me out of all recognition, in a way that I couldn't possibly have anticipated.

# II

I'd thought, when I first arrived there, that university was the closest thing to utopia that I was ever likely to find in England's not-very-green and not-very-pleasant land, and I wasn't wrong. It was a very relaxed and undemanding environment, and by 1999 the balance of the sexes among the student population had almost reached the parity that's now taken for granted. Males were still a majority in physics, maths, law and economics, but in sociology the that unbalance was reversed, not as much as in English, but enough to make it seem that it was the kind of environment in which even a medium-sized and not particularly good-looking bloke like me, who didn't even own a car, could get laid—and so it proved. While far from being a campus stud, it only took a couple of months of angling for me to form a steady and satisfactory relationship with Alison.

Similar arithmetic suggested to me, from the very beginning, that even though the actual work in the call center was far more tedious and much more time-consuming, the place might well have one utopian advantage even greater than uni: the fact that females were in such a large majority that it was rare for any particular day-shift crew to have more than three blokes working alongside twenty nubile females. In a competitive environment like that, I thought, almost as soon as I sat down at my unit—we didn't have offices, of course, and didn't even have a regular desk, being assigned a position depending on availability when we clocked on—even a sweeper with lead boots could score at regular intervals. It didn't take long, however, to encounter the downside of the situation.

It wasn't that the lasses weren't up for it. Quite the reverse, in fact, with regard to the teenagers. I doubt that there was one among them who hadn't lost her virginity at thirteen and taken to the sport like a duck to water, but they certainly didn't play by the rules that I'd got used to at the university. Maybe it was a side effect of the working environment and maybe it was just a sign of the times, but the majority didn't seem to bother with "dating" or "relationships" at all. The principal focal point of their social lives seemed to be weekly "girls' nights out," on which they'd go out in gaggles of eight or ten, drinking like fish and laughing like lunatics with one another, until the time came to go home, at which time, if they happened to fancy a shag, they'd hook up with someone who happened to be convenient, depending on the circumstances of the moment—not that much different from the unit-allocation system at work, in fact.

I'm not sure even to this day to what extent that subculture was localized—forgive me for talking like a sociologist, but I've never quite managed to kick the habit—either geographically or occupationally, but I do know that it had certain idiosyncratic twists at the Scott Hall Road centre. All stereotyped subcultures tend to develop such mutations in individual locales, of course, and the factors differentiating particular workplaces from the standard pattern are always associated with particular role models: individuals possessed of a degree of what the technical jargon calls charisma. Every hen party needs an alpha-female to set the tone and the pace, and to lay down a particular philosophy of procedure, and the standard pattern of behavior at the girl's nights out ventured by the staff of the Scott Hall Road center had been largely determined, perhaps not surprisingly, by the best-looking staffer, whose name was Trudi Hemming.

Trudi had been in the center since day one, and she must have been slightly older than the rest of that original intake as well as far better looking. She was my age rather than a teenager, and she had, so to speak, been around a bit—to put it mildly. By the time I arrived, as the oldest member of a new bunch of fresh-faced recruits, and the only male therein, she was already a legend, and not merely in Scott Hall Road.

I started on a Monday, and by Wednesday, I had already been taken under the wing of one of the other ex-uni staffers, Jez, who seemed glad of my advent and more than ready to welcome me as a blood-brother in the B.A. fraternity. Human Resources, who actually had an office on site where three older women worked—also in shifts, so that only two were there at any one time—must have fixed things, in order to ease my introduction to the workplace proper, so that I was working the same section of the same shift as Jez for my first three days, and thus taking my breaks at much the same time, in order that he could easily give me all the information I desperately needed but that no training program could possibly provide.

I say "much the same time" because the break system was slightly dependent on calls; if you were in mid-call when your break-time came up, you had to finish the call first, and with some of our callers, that could easily use up half, or even all, of the notional time. The time you lost was then added on, of course—the whole process was calculated by computer and signaled by flashing indicator-lights—but it meant that breaks could easily get slightly out of phase. Because of the way the system worked, of course, all breaks had to be staggered; only ten per cent of the workers on shift could be away from the phones at any moment, so each shift was broken up into sections, with the result that even at peak times during the day shifts only three or four people were likely to be on their break simultaneously—and the simultaneity was, as I've just explained, a trifle approximate.

You might not think that people whose work consists of sitting at desk chatting on the phone would need a lot of breaks, but again, you'd be wrong. The level of concentration required to handle one customer after another, usually with no more than a five-second interval between calls, while sticking rigidly to all the protocols, never becoming flustered, and always being scrupulously polite, is actually very taxing. Human Resources policy, doubtless armed with the results of scrupulous research, had calculated that maximum productivity was maintained if the workers had fifteen minutes of break per ninety minutes of gross shift-time, so that in a standard seven-and-a-half-hour shift you got four breaks, three in a six-hour shift and five in a nine-hour shift. There were no longer breaks—no "lunch time"—but the Management kindly provided a snack machine right next to the coffee machine and doubtless a regulation distance from the doors of the loos. Not many people used it, though—you could get cheaper crisps and chocolate at the supermarket, and sandwiches too.

I don't know the extent to which the necessity of catering to addicted smokers figured into the fifteen-minutes-in-ninety calculation, but it was certainly the case that the majority of the staffers at Scott Hall Road immediately made a bee-line for the door when the time for their break came up, in order to get outside and have a fag even before heading for the loo. Smoking in public places hadn't yet been banned by law in 1999, but it was forbidden in most workplaces, and the Scott Hall Road Management liked to think of themselves as being ahead of the curve in every respect. That tended to leave the sofa beside the coffee-machine almost as deserted as the Gents, unless the roll of the dice brought two non-smokers together. Jez and I were never the only non-smokers sharing overlapping shifts, but in that first week, we were usually the only non-smokers on the shift taking our breaks simultaneously, and usually had the sofa to ourselves.

The first few breaks we shared on that system were almost exclusively devoted to tips about the practicalities of the work but it didn't take long, naturally, for him to start giving me as much dope as he had on the girls. The logic of the situation suggested that he ought to start with the ones on the overlapping shifts that we could presently see, and he could actually point out, but Trudi's name came up a full two days before I was actually able to clap eyes on her.

"Come Friday, mate," Jez said, "Trudi will probably invite you to go out for a drink with the girls. She'll be on the same shift as you in the afternoon, so it's a virtual certainty. You'd be invited eventually anyway, so that the girls can sound you out, but it's Trudi's prerogative to make the first move, so they always leave it to her if she's on in time."

"Okay," I said. "Any reason why I shouldn't accept?"

"Absolutely not," he told me. "That wouldn't be a good idea at all. It's a kind of ritual that you have to go through—a sort of initiation. But you'll need a few tips, if you're to come through it unscathed."

"You've been through it, of course?"

"Absolutely. They call them girls' nights out, and they sometimes tell the blokes to steer clear, but usually, it's easy enough to tag along if you want to, with one group or another—at least, it is if you get the thumbs-up from Trudi, so it will help if you can make a good impression on Friday."

"And how do I do that?"

"God only knows, mate—and that's the first thing you have to take aboard. However it goes, don't take it personally. She's a moody cow even at the best of times, but when she's putting some poor bloke through his paces she's completely unpredictable. She's a real…do you happen know what the female equivalent of a misogynist is?"

"A misandrist?"

"If that means someone who's got a prejudice against blokes that makes the average Yorkshireman's prejudice against skirts look weak-kneed, yes. That doesn't mean she doesn't fuck, mind—to listen her, you'd think she's laid half the male population of Yorkshire, end to end—but it does mean that it's not the kind of encounter you can to go into expecting an easy ride. The ride you might well get, if you play your cards right—not that I can tell you what that will require, on the night—but it won't be easy."

He was obviously speaking from experience, but I didn't know him well enough then to press him for intimate details, and our time was up anyway of that particular break. When the conversation resumed, seventy-five minutes later or thereabouts, I stuck to simple prompts, and let him explain it in his own way.

"The thing is, mate," he said. "it's easy to arrange to be one of the blokes on one of the nights that the slags are willing to invite one or more of their male colleagues to join them on their riotous nights off, and if you stick with them all night you're practically guaranteed to cop off with someone—but there's a price to be paid, and Trudi kind of sets the tariff, not just for tickets to her own dubious favors, but in a general sort of way. The others look up to her, see? They copy her, because they mostly want to be like her, even if they don't really have the looks for it, or the iron constitution."

"Right," I said, encouragingly.

"What I mean is that even if they like you, and actually quite want to fuck you, they'll put you through the wringer first. When you're out with the girls, you have put up with a lot of…well, they call it joking, but it's mostly just vulgar abuse. It's mostly about men in general, but it's likely to get gradually more personal as the booze goes down, especially if Trudi's there. If you want to get laid, odds are that the only thing you have to do is grit your teeth and stick it out—taking it in good part, they call that—but the other thing you have to bear in mind is that you won't be able to choose. They'll do the choosing. I don't know how they do it, but by the time the evening ends, and they're all off their faces, they'll have worked out between themselves which of them gets the prize, and you have to like it or lump it. My advice is either to duck out early, or to like it, however it turn out; it's like they say about asking for credit—a refusal often offends. Even ducking out early can be hazardous—they're likely to conclude that you're a bit short in the ball department, and it might cause something of a drought in future invitations. On the other hand, if you get so drunk that you can't perform, and that rumor goes around…same difference."

There was obviously a lot to think about, and I wasn't at all sure that it was a subculture in which I wanted to involve myself wholeheartedly or at length. So I asked the logical question.

"Is that the only way to get laid around here?"

Jez pulled a face. "Pretty much," he said. "Not all the girls who work here play the game, obviously, but the ones who don't almost all have regular boyfriends and take their relationships seriously, and the rest tend to try to keep work and personal life completely separate."

At subsequent breaks, we ran through a dozen visible examples, which Jez obligingly located within his classification system, but I had to ask him about the only one that had really caught my eye.

"What about the little goth girl over there on the left?"

"Sheena? Never goes on girl's nights out, but has a regular boy-friend. Weird, anyway. Also has a lot of time off; I'll be surprised if she doesn't get the sack before long."

"Why weird?" I asked. "Or do you just mean the goth look?"

"It's not just the look, mate," Jez assured me. "She's deeply into it—and not just the music. Some of the girls think she's completely off her head, although Trudi, to be fair, always sticks up for her, and won't let anyone take a pop at her. Knows her big sister, I think. Anyway, she's pretty much off limits. Why, do you like the goth look?"

"Yes, I do," I said.

"Well, she's dressed for work right now," he said, "but those are actually her civvies. Nights out, she has her hair in spikes, eyes made up like fireworks and all the silver jewelry, studded armbands and all. Wouldn't be so bad, I suppose, if it were only the outfit, but she's a vampire goth—not just an Anne Rice fan, but a full-blown pretender, so it's said. The girls reckon that she learned to hypnotize herself so she could access her past lives, and maybe she did, because she doesn't really seem to be living in the present. A mate of mine who knew her at school told me her name's really Susan—they all make up names, although they usually pick something classier than Sheena. Knowing how the girls exaggerate, she's probably not actually crazy, but as I said, she does takes more time off than the others. Bad legs, apparently."

"I'm surprised there aren't more goths on the staff—Leeds was goth central once upon a time."

"That was way back in the eighties and the heyday of the Sisters. Things move fast in music, and they've changed a lot while you've been away down south. Still a lot of goths about, mind, just not in the call center game. Doesn't really fit the image, seen from either side. I can tell you where the crowd hangs out nowadays, if you want—but you'll need to get more gothed up yourself if you want to infiltrate. Just dressing in black the way you are now won't cut it. It's pretty exclusive."

I knew that; I'd toyed with the idea of further emphasis before I went away, when the Sisters of Mercy were still my favorite easy listening and hadn't yet become passé, and I'd already got the habit of dressing in black chinos, a black shirt and a black jacket, but I hadn't had the courage to dye my hair black while I was still at school, let alone deck myself out in faux-silver jewelry and studded leather armbands, and down south, the subculture didn't have much extension outside London, so uni had been a virtually goth-free zone.

I did like the look, though, and I was glad, on the Thursday, when the arcane workings of the shift system provided me with a coincidence with the goth girl's breaks. She didn't smoke either, so we met at the coffee machine.

"Hi," I said to her. "I'm Kirk Markham."

She looked me up and down, appraising me while I appraised her. She was small—no more than five-two—and thin rather than slender, with a facial pallor that was entirely natural, further heightened by the black hair and eye make-up, but her eyes were pale blue. I couldn't tell what she thought of me—she gave no obvious signs of approval or disapproval—but I thought she was gorgeous.

"Sheena," she said.

That was when I made my first mistake. "Is that your real name?" I asked. I knew as soon as the words were out of my mouth that it was a *faux pas*, but my mouth always tended to run faster than mature reflection in those days.

Her lip curled scornfully. "Of course it is," she said—which meant, I suppose, that although it wasn't, any suggestion to the effect that she might really be a Susan would be considered to be in rank bad taste.

"Right," I said, and swiftly moved to safer ground. "Have you been working here long?"

"Nearly two years. I started not long after leaving school." I took the voluntary addition of the second sentence as a good sign; obviously I hadn't blotted my copy-book irredeemably.

"I've just started, I said, stating the obvious, and added, by way of symmetry: "I've just left university."

"What did you study?" she asked—another good sign.

"Sociology," I admitted.

Mercifully, she didn't laugh or look down her nose. "I think I'd have liked to do English," she said, "but I missed too much school, and couldn't get the grades."

"I couldn't get good enough grades to do English either," I said, a trifle wistfully. "Never missed any school but didn't focus enough on the syllabus. Always read a lot, but always the wrong books. Sociology had lower grade requirements: the road of least resistance. My old headmaster told me once, when he was telling me off for shirking, that people who always take the road of least resistance never get anywhere in life, but he always talked in clichés—it wasn't a special occasion."

"And yet here you are," she said, lightly. "Scott Hall Road call center—the acme of anyone's ambition." She kept her face straight, but her blue eyes sparkled ever so slightly. I remember that. I think I always will. The fact that she'd used the phrase "acme of ambition" set her apart; she was obviously a reader too, if only of the wrong books.

The next time the indicator light thrust us together, I became garrulous: "I'm really impressed by the way that the people working here manage to develop an artificial multiple personality. It's as if they become a completely different person when they're on the phone—an altered state of consciousness that they can just switch on and off."

"You're exaggerating," she replied—it wasn't the first time that accusation had been leveled against me—"and even to the extent that it's true, it's perfectly normal. People act differently at work and at home, changing as they move from one social environment to another."

"I'm supposed to be the sociologist," I told her. "You're getting dangerously close to trespassing on my intellectual territory."

"Sorry," she said. "I didn't realize that a degree gave you the monopoly. Are you Steve Markham's little brother?"

"Yes," I said. "Why, do you know him?"

"No," she said, "but we have mutual acquaintances. He's in the army now?"

"That's right," I said. "Posted abroad—Kosovo. Won't see him for a while, alas."

She nodded.

"What mutual acquaintances?" I asked, curiously.

She looked me in the eyes, but I couldn't tell from her expression what reaction she was looking for, or what she expected, when she said: "It was Trudi Hemming who mentioned him to me. You won't have met her yet, but she'll be on this shift tomorrow."

I racked my brains trying to remember whether Steve had ever mentioned the notorious Trudi; I was pretty sure that he hadn't. Suddenly, it seemed that I'd been away for a long time. If she really had laid half the males in Leeds, at least in the appropriate age-group, though, it wouldn't have been that surprising if Steve had been on the list. He was taller and better-looking than me, and if the army had finished making a man of him, it had had good raw material with which to start. He wasn't the kind of person always to take the road of least resistance.

My heart sank somewhat. If my moral credit at the Center was dependent on Trudi's assessment, and she started out by comparing me to my brother…but then, what had she thought of him, if, as Jez said, she was a misandrist through and through?"

Sheena was still watching me. "I gather that you've heard of Trudi?" she said. "From Jez, I suppose?"

"Yes," I admitted, warily.

"He warned you about what he calls the initiation ceremony?"

"Yes," I admitted, even more warily.

"Don't take him too seriously," she advised, seemingly motivated by pure kindness. "Trudi's not really the gorgon she pretends to be—but for God's sake don't tell her I told you that."

I would have liked to follow up on that, but our not-quite-fifteen minutes was up again. I hadn't yet got used to maintaining continuity in conversations carved up into segments like that.

# III

As promised, my Friday shift overlapped with Trudi Hemming's, although I started a couple of hours earlier. For the first couple of breaks I was coincident with Jez, but his shift had started two hours before mine, so he left before I finished. In theory, I should have been alone on the sofa for my final break, because Trudi was a smoker, but she was obviously in control of her addiction, because when her call finished she made a bee-line for me instead if the door.

"You're Kirk?" she said, wasting no time, obviously well-accustomed to fragmented conversation.

"Yes," I said. I wanted to say more, but the burden of accumulated intimation was too great.

"Trudi Hemming," she said, studying me, watching for the reaction. She was the same height as me, but the way her eyes were boring into me made me feel somewhat smaller. Her eyes were blue, but not as pale as Sheena's, although not exactly royal blue either. Her hair was a rich amber blonde, which was more than half her charm, although her face was nicely symmetrical and her complexion, though healthy, wasn't overly red. She was smiling—quite pleasantly, it seemed to me, although I was worried about the possible naivety of taking appearances for granted.

I must have hesitated, because she didn't wait for a verbal reaction. "It's okay," she said. "You needn't bother with the 'I've heard a lot about you,' and I know that Jez has already warned you about me, but I hope you won't take what he says too seriously. Some of the girls and I are going on for a drink when my shift finishes, and we wondered if you'd care to join us. I know you finish at four, so it'll mean coming back into town, but if that's not too much of a fag, come along, any time between six and seven. We'll be in the Black Boar, and we'd be glad to have you join us, so we can welcome you aboard. Okay?"

"Fine," I said. "It'll be nice to have a conversation that lasts longer than not-quite-fifteen minutes for once."

"I can't guarantee that," she said, still smiling, "but we'll do our best, in the interests of getting to know you."

"Thanks," I said. She was already turning away, evidently not in that much control over her addiction, when I said: "You know my brother?"

The ghost of a frown creased her forehead, ever so slightly, perhaps because she didn't know whether Sheena had told me that, or whether Steve might have mentioned her.

"It's a big city," she told me, "but our little corner of it is fairly tight. Lots of people know lots of people—unless they go down south to study sociology." Evidently, she already knew quite a lot about me.

"That's true," I admitted, in a neutral tone. "I guess I'll have to re-adapt as best I can. I'll mention to Steve that I've met you next time I get a chance to talk to him on the phone. Shall I give him your regards?"

The smile broadened—but not, I thought, with gratitude. "Please do," she said, without overmuch irony in her tone—but she looked at me a little more sharply with her lovely blue eyes, and I couldn't help wondering whether I'd just made another *faux pas*, for which I might have to pay later in the evening, when we got to know one another a little bit better.

I did go back to the flat after my shift finished, but not to make any elaborate preparations for my night out. If the girls were going straight from work they would presumably be doing no more than tarting up their make-up a little, and I didn't want to seem to be making too much effort. I took a reasonable quantity of cash, in case the round I expected to have to buy turned out to be mind-bogglingly expensive, but left my credit card at home.

The Black Boar was no longer the bog-standard pub it had once been, having been carefully gentrified by the chain that had bought it into a "wine bar," but the present owners had been careful to keep the name and the old sign, because they constituted "character," which was considered to be a marketable commodity, especially as the interior was so obviously devoid of it.

The girls had already been drinking for a while when I got there, a little bit late even though I'd taken the bus, and the round I bought turned out to be quite modestly priced, as they were only drinking wine, not bizarre cocktails.

At first, it seemed that Jez had been exaggerating wildly, because the general conversation was almost entirely focused on work, and all the awkward clients that the girls had had to cope with during the previous week's shifts, and the questions that we put to me, from various directions and in some abundance, were simply fact-gathering questions of a perfectly innocuous sort. Nobody mentioned Steve, but one of the younger girls, Maxine, who had also started that week and had been invited along in the same way I had, knew Lily slightly from school, and must presumably have been aware of me too in the same context, although we had been years apart, and people at school are always likely to be more aware of people ahead of them than people behind them. Because the same sorts of questions were directed at her as were being directed at me, I learned more about her than any of her companions, who all knew one another already. She was a trifle timid, but quite sweet.

For the first couple of hours, it wouldn't have been obvious at a glance that Trudi was in charge—she didn't make the slightest attempt to dominate or steer the conversation—but it gradually became evident, by virtue of the way that the others continually looked at her obliquely in search of approval, that she was the person who really mattered.

"What sort of job are you looking for?" Maxine asked me, when I'd gone through the customary rigmarole about how the call center was only a stopgap, and that I didn't expect to be there more than a few months.

"I don't really know," I confessed. "Teaching is out. I suppose, like everyone else, I'd like to get into the media, but the competition is way too stiff, and I've spoiled my record somewhat by gathering a reputation as a non-trier. I think I'll have to try to make a better impression at the center, so that I can get more helpful reference."

"Good luck with that," said one of the others, a pretty brunette named Rachel. "I've been trying to get out for a while, but nobody seems to take much notice of the references, and the fact that you've been in a center seems to put people off a bit. HR people in other outfits don't appreciate how much skill there is in our job."

"That's a pity," I commiserated, and repeated what I'd told Sheena about admiring the way that they became so skilled at switching personalities at the drop of a hat. If I'd timed the comment better they could have qualified as famous last words, but that was still some way ahead of the switch being pressed that turned them all into bloodthirsty maenads. There was a way to go yet, as the comments about the clients who phoned up became gradually more abusive, and more misandrist.

Unlike the staffers, of course, who were ninety per cent female, the people who rang the call center seemed to be ninety per cent male, presumably because males tend to be early adopters of new gadgets, and almost all of the apparatus that the company was marketing still qualified as new gadgetry, not having yet become familiar aspects of the workplace landscape. Also, males are far more ready to complain if they can't get something to work, and far more likely to get frustrated and angry if the problem they're blaming on someone else isn't sorted out pronto.

I mention that by way of admission that the staffers' misandry was, to a large extent, at least in that initial manifesto, perfectly justified. As their comments about particular rude and stupid individuals were slowly transformed into general judgments abut the general boorishness and incompetence of the male fraction of the population, there was a lot of sociological common sense in what they were saying, and I didn't have much difficulty in agreeing with most of it, even when it edged into discussion of the way men typically handled—or, rather, typically mishandled—personal relationships.

People were constantly moving around and swapping places, so I didn't immediately notice when Maxine, who had been sitting next to me, was replaced by Trudi, and didn't think anything of it when I did notice. While not exactly drunk, I was quite relaxed by then, and somewhat off guard.

The hazing—or ordeal, or whatever one might care to call it—didn't begin immediately, even then. The first thing Trudi said to me that was of any significance, in fact, was: "I hear you were chatting up Sheena Howell yesterday."

I could simply have said "So what?" but there didn't seem to be any reason to be aggressive, especially in the context of the conversation, so what I actually said was: "I wasn't *chatting her up*, just chatting. Jez told me she's got a steady boyfriend."

She looked at me oddly, as if wondering whether, in view of that answer, she might have done better to keep quiet. "Jez is behind the times," she said, after a pause. "They've broken up. She might be a bit vulnerable at the moment. Tread carefully, will you?"

I remembered what Jez had said about Trudi not allowing anyone to "take a pop" at Sheena, and wondered exactly what the phrase was intended to imply.

"She seemed perfectly serene to me," I said. "We were just chatting; I didn't say anything that she could take amiss." And I carefully didn't add that it was none of her business.

She probably noticed the omission. "I know her sister," she said, as if by way of explanation. "She works at Gap."

I nodded, as if it were, in fact, an explanation, and a perfectly satisfactory one.

"So, Kirk," she said, without transition, although the switch had obviously been flicked, "do you want to fuck me."

There was no obvious *coup de théâtre*. The general conversation didn't stop. Silence didn't fall. From the corner of my eye, I saw a startled expression on Maxine's face, but Rachel and the others didn't blink. They didn't even seem to be watching us, but they were. I knew that we were the center of attention, and that the trial had begun. I'd been warned. I'd had time to think about it, and even though I hadn't been at the call center long enough, as yet to know how to switch personalities at the drop of a hat, my previous relaxation didn't leave me floundering, unable to figure out how to react.

I met her blue gaze steadily, and replied, as if it were the most natural answer in the world to the most natural question in the world: "I don't know yet."

"You don't know?" Her tone was perfectly level, without the slightest hint of resentment or wrath. "Here's my face"—she pointed at it, just in case I didn't know where she meant—"And here are my tits"—likewise—"what more do you need to know? You can stick your hand in my knickers if you want, to test out the rest of the equipment."

"That's all right," I said. "I'm sure it's in perfect order. I just meant that I don't really know you very well."

"Bullshit," she said. "You're a man. You know perfectly well after one glance whether you want to fuck someone or not, so answer the fucking question."

I gathered my theoretical resources. They were ready to hand, because I'd figured I might need them, and I wasn't drunk; the relaxation, I figured, would probably help.

"Obviously," I said, "You're extremely attractive, and doubtless perfectly correct in the assumption that every straight bloke between the ages of thirteen and ninety-three would find the idea of fucking you extremely tempting—but one could say the same for all the women here present, and in order to decide, in practical terms, who one might actually want to fuck, or try to fuck, one has to make a decision based on more than mere appearance. So the answer is that I really don't know you well enough, as yet, to make a firm decision. I hope you can forgive my uncertainty—I assure you that I don't mean any offense."

"Fucking sociology graduate," she said, making me wish that I had a pound for every time I'd heard that particular insult. "Fucking bullshit. You don't know? No balls, if you ask me."

I hadn't asked her, but I let that pass, and searched for the road of least resistance.

"Just like Goebbels," I said. Actually, I said it completely absent-mindedly, almost reflexively. It wasn't an argumentative ploy, intended to put her off her stride—but it did put her off her stride. She was young; she had left school at sixteen; she didn't watch the History Channel; she genuinely had no idea who Goebbels was.

"Who the fuck is Goebbels?" she said. That too was a reflex, not an argumentative ploy. She didn't know and she didn't like not knowing. She didn't like the suspicion that I might be taking the piss out of her.

"Sorry," I said. "It's from a song my granddad used to sing, back in the eighties, before he died. He had senile dementia, you see. He couldn't remember anything recent, maybe not for thirty or forty years, but he still had flashes of memory from the forties, especially the war, and especially songs. He didn't know who I was, or Mum, or Steve, when we went to see him in the nursing home, but he could still sing the choruses of Vera Lynn songs, and especially comic songs from his air force days—he was ground crew, a mechanic. He used to sing a song about Flying Fortresses and Avro Lancasters to the tune of the Battle Hymn of the Republic, and he used to sing another to the tune of Colonel Bogey, which went: *Hitler has only got one ball; Goering has two but very small; Himmler is very sim'lar, but Goebbels has no balls at all*. Goebbels was Hitler's minister of propaganda."

"I've heard that!" Rachel put in, helpfully.

Trudi didn't say anything. She had lost the thread of her assault—but the reason I kept talking wasn't because I thought it was a good idea not to let her take it up again; I just got carried away talking about granddad.

"It was strange," I said, "seeing him in those last few months. His eyesight was very poor—macular degeneration—but when you lose much of your visual field, you brain doesn't like to admit it, so when you look at people, when your retina doesn't pick up enough information to identify them, the brain improvises—makes a guess, I suppose—except that granddad's memory was shot to hell, so the faces it filled in, the people he thought he was looking at, were people from forty years before. Not necessarily people he'd known that well, so far as I could gather, but just people who happened to make an impression at the time. I was only a kid then, of course, but I had a vivid imagination, and I couldn't help wondering who I might see when I was old, half-blind and half-witted. Maybe one of the things that will stick will be this moment, and maybe one of the people I'll see, sixty years from now, when everything between now and then has just faded into a gray mist, will be you, Trudi, or you, Rachel. I daren't hope, obviously, that you might see me, because I'm not that memorable, but I might well see you, no matter what decision I eventually come to on the question you asked."

In a way, that was quite a compliment, and they all sensed that, although they all suspected, as anyone would be bound to do, that it was mere flattery, of the sort that is proverbially supposed to get you anywhere. It wasn't flattery; I actually meant it, as a hypothetical possibility. I really wasn't trying to get into Trudi's knickers although I'm not entirely sure even to this day why I wasn't. Logically, and rationally, I should have been, given that I was not, in fact, akin to the fictitious Goebbels of the malevolent song. I'd like to think that it was the news that Sheena Howell didn't, after all, have a steady boyfriend that had made me pause, but I suspect that it had more to do with the lurking suspicion that Trudi had fucked my big brother, and was already making comparisons that were unlikely, at any point in time, to work to my advantage.

"God," said Trudi," you really do talk a lot of bullshit, don't you?" The absence of any emphatic expletives seemed to indicate that she was mellowing, and that some of the force had gone out of her assault.

"Sociology graduate," I said, with a sigh. "I can't help it. Women down south don't necessarily find it unattractive, but now I'm back in Yorkshire, where the lasses are blunter than a hack's pencil, I guess it's not going to cut any ice, butter any parsnips or mix any metaphors."

"That line actually works down south, does it?" Trudi asked, perhaps even genuinely interested in the variance of sexual mores in various parts of the United Kingdom. "You're not actually a virgin, then?"

"Not exactly," I replied, with an equally contrived sigh.

"*Not exactly?* What's that supposed to mean?"

"It means that I've tested the equipment, and it works, but that I haven't progressed beyond mere orgasms to authentic exaltation."

"That's a fancy way of saying that you've had sex, but never been *in love?*" I had never before heard anyone pronounce the phrase "in love" with so much utter contempt, as if it were filthier, in its fashion, than the worst of expletives. By this time, our dialogue was the only one still continuing within the circle, and the others were listening with frank attention.

"I've fooled myself briefly a time or two," I admitted, "but it's like everything else—it takes practice. I think I might be able to do it now, if the opportunity arose."

"Come off it," she said. "You're a bloke—all you care about is dipping your wick. That *love* bullshit is just a line, a story made up to fool women into thinking that there's more to sex for men than masturbation with a live sex-toy."

"You could be right," I conceded, "but I haven't given up hope yet." I looked around the circle, to emphasize that the next question wasn't just meant for Trudi, and said: "Have you?"

Even Trudi didn't simply affirm it. "It's bullshit," she said. "Pie in the sky. All lies and dressing up."

Women, of course, ought to apply the Claud Cockburn principle even more ruthlessly and cynically than journalists and newspaper-readers, especially to men trying to get into their knickers—but it didn't seem to be an apposite time to add that observation to the argumentative mix.

"Perhaps it is," I agreed, "But as I say, I haven't given up hope yet. Perhaps it comes of reading too many books, or taking too many of them too seriously, but I'd like to think that there's something more to be obtained from relationships between men and women than brute intercourse. Perhaps the entire mythology of love is just a fantasy, but if so, it's surely a necessary fantasy, and there's no advantage, in terms of human wellbeing, in losing the illusion. Quite the reverse, in fact. You've accused me of talking bullshit, and perhaps I am, but not all bullshit of that kind stinks. When I say that I won't know whether I want to fuck you, or anyone else here present, until I know you, or them, a little better, maybe I'm fooling myself, and maybe it's just lack of balls that makes me hesitate, but I don't think it is, and if I'm deluded, I'd really rather you didn't try so insistently to disillusion me. It isn't kind."

"It isn't supposed to be *kind*," said Trudi, although she didn't put quite as much disgust into the word *kind* as she'd previously out into the word *love*. I remembered what Sheena had said about her not really being the gorgon she pretended to be.

"I'd gathered that," I said, quietly. "As you said this afternoon, you invited me here in order to get to know me, and in order that I could get to know you." Again, I scanned the circle. "Are we making progress, do you think?"

She laughed. I honestly couldn't tell whether that seemed to her to be a natural consequence of the momentum of the contest, or whether she's pressed the switch and changed personalities again. "I guess we are," she said. "Okay, you're off the hook. I'll settle for 'I don't know.' Thousands wouldn't, mind, and if you really want to score in these parts you'll have to develop a better line than that. I wouldn't have fucked you anyway. It was a hypothetical question, not a proposition."

"I gathered that, too," I said, truthfully.

She wasn't going to leave it without a sting in the tail, though. "And nobody else round here is going to fuck you until you've got your act together," she added—and it was her turn to parade her gaze around the circle, as if issuing a royal edict.

I hadn't made a deep enough impression on any of them for any of them even to think of rebelling against the edict, but the argument I'd formulated, somewhat at hazard, had presumably eliminated the possibility anyway. I estimated, however, that I had probably passed the examination, in the same way that I had passed all my previous examinations, with the aid of fluency and trusting to luck. I wasn't even too drunk, when the party broke up, to find my back home—which was perhaps as well, as no one volunteered to escort me, so if I'd collapsed *en route* I'd have had to rely on the ever-dubious kindness of strangers.

# IV

I had the same shift on Saturday, with the same overlaps, so Jez was able to take possession of me at my first break.

"How did you get on last night?" he asked. "Did you score?"

"No," I told him. "I think I accidentally managed to talk my way out of it, while fending off Trudi's gibes, but I think I came through more-or-less unscathed. Have you heard any talk?"

"A couple of remarks," he admitted. "Nothing specific, but I got the idea that they think you're okay—which isn't bad. We college boys generally have to work a little harder to impress them. Generally, they prefer rugby players."

"Or soldiers," I supplied, almost inaudibly.

He didn't ask me to repeat it. "Don't imagine you'll be accepted as a full member of the gang, though," he went on. "That doesn't happen. The problem with being a male hanger-on on a girls' night out in Leeds is that it's a bit like being a male stripper at a hen party—in fact, you have to be careful that it doesn't turn out exactly like that. They were probably being careful last night, in fact, because they didn't know you. Once they feel free to take liberties…well you can work it out. You'll always be the butt of all the banter, and the talk will always get filthier with every unit of alcohol that's sunk. The suggestive remarks, the lewd questions and the probing fingers will become increasingly intrusive and increasingly aggressive. But there are compensations, as I said."

I knew what he meant by compensations, but I wasn't sure that I wanted compensations of that essentially drunken and fundamentally contemptuous sort, even with Trudi's hair and eyes thrown in, or the more modest attractions possessed by at least half the other girls.

"It's not just that they're mimicking what they see as the essential features of lad culture," Jez went on—he was a graduate too, albeit in so-called media studies--"which would be more than bad enough, believe me, but that while they're doing it they feel that they're getting their own back for thousands of years of indignity heaped upon their mothers, grandmothers and so on, all the way back to Eve. Because of that, lasses don't go over the top in the kind of easygoing, natural way that blokes do. In over-the-top terms, every girls' night out is the second day of the

Somme and the troops aren't usually in any mood for taking prisoners. It isn't so bad, though, if you can just grit your teeth and wait for the payoff at the end."

The way he kept harping on about that made me suspect a certain measure of desperate optimism.

"Maybe so," I said, figuring that a little moral support wouldn't come amiss, "but if you don't get to choose which of the witches will eventually take you home, it's all a bit tacky, isn't it? For anyone with an ounce of sensibility, like you or me, the path to that kind of consummation is a trifle thorny."

"Too right," he agreed, seemingly relieved that I'd implied that any failure on his part could only be interpreted as a compliment to his sensitivity. "Some blokes come out of it really badly, though, and you have to feel sorry for them. Even for blokes, pull-a-pig contests are a bit disgusting, but when lasses start, it gets positively horrific. After two hours of listening to those kinds of reminiscences, no man alive could get any kind of kick out of scoring, even if it happens to be the one he actually fancies who eventually drags him off. No matter what she whispers in his ear when they're finally alone, he always feels like a prize porker ripe for the Polaroid laugh track."

I could see what he meant. The conversation hadn't degenerated to that extent the previous night, but it was as well to know that it might, if I were tempted to repeat the experiment.

Perhaps surprisingly, when I we got to the break after Jez had left, Trudi didn't immediately head for the door. Instead, she came over to me and said. "Don't just sit around on the sofa on your own. Come outside and talk to me while I have a fag."

Meekly, I obeyed.

"Did you enjoy yourself last night," she asked, with an expression of perfect innocence.

"Yes, I did," I said, heroically. "It was quite entertaining to see you all getting your own back for ten thousand years of male chauvinism—but I'm not sure I could stand the ego-battering on a routine basis."

She nodded, as if it were a perfectly reasonable response. There was barely a pause before she said: "I know that you were just trying to fend me off, but what you said about your grandfather—that was true, wasn't it?"

"Every word," I confirmed.

I thought she was just fishing for a compliment by recalling what I'd said about her possibly making enough impression to survive the ravages of senile dementia, but she wasn't.

"And you really think about things like that?" she said. "What it might be like when you get old and lose your marbles?"

"Difficult not to, when you have an example in front of you," I said.

"You could have forgotten it, given that it was more than ten years ago," she pointed out, and added: "I don't think about it. I don't even think about what it will be like when my face falls off and nobody wants to fuck me any more. I try to live in the moment."

I couldn't resist, "*Carpe diem*, as Messalina would have said."

"You just can't help it, can't you?" she said, apparently more in sorrow than anger. "All right, who the fuck is Messalina?"

I was actually quite surprised that she didn't know.

"Wife of the Roman Emperor Claudius," I said. "Fifty years after she was dead, two so-called historians who had a political interest in blackening his dynasty published a slanderous account of his reign, which was actually the most successful in Roman history, heaping all kinds of abuse on him, claiming that he was a drooling idiot whose wife had cuckolded him with half the male population of the city. Later tattlers added the allegation that Messalina worked pseudonymously in a brothel and engaged in sex competitions with the professional whores. All lies, but the force of legend being what it is, she was permanently stuck with the reputation of being the ultimate slut."

She could hardly miss the subtext, but she didn't seem to take offense. "How do you know it's all lies?" she asked.

She had me there. "I don't," I admitted. "I just assumed."

"And you think you're paying the poor woman a compliment by assuming that?"

"I did think exactly that," I admitted. "But perhaps that says more about me than her."

"That's what I thought," she said. "Have you made up your mind yet? In fact, no—on second thoughts, it doesn't matter, since I'm not going to fuck you whatever you decide. You'll probably think that's a compliment to me, although it actually says more about you."

"Ouch," I said. "Is it going to be like this every time you talk to me? It's a high price to pay for the occasional privilege of watching you poison yourself slowly one fag at a time."

"Sorry," she said, unrepentantly. "I thought you were enjoying yourself. Would you really rather I was *kind*?"

I had to think about that one for a few seconds. "I suppose not," I said. "You won't mind me nursing the illusion that you don't really mean it, I hope?"

"Wouldn't want it any other way," she assured me.

I decided to believe her.

* * * *

Sunday was my day off, so I went to have lunch with Mum and Lily. I gave them a severely bowdlerized account of what working at the call center was like, and mentioned to Lily that some of our old school fellows were there, more her age than mine. She remembered Maxine, but only vaguely; they hadn't been in the same form. "But it's just a stopgap," I said. "They'll go on to better things."

"I might end up working there myself," she said, in no particular tone.

I could hardly protest, but the idea of Lily at one of those girls' nights out made me shudder. She was seventeen, and the calculus of probability suggested that she was probably no longer a virgin, but she was my little sister, and that was another of the illusions that I wanted to preserve, at least for a little while longer. I wanted her to go to university, become a doctor, marry a fellow doctor and live happily ever after in respectable suburbia.

Mum was much more concerned with whether the flat was being cleaned properly and whether I was getting my laundry done. The thought that I not only didn't own an ironing board but didn't even think that the omission was an important lifestyle error was something that caused her a measure of sorrow and horror. I assured her that I was eating properly, not living on junk food, and that I got the vacuum cleaner out regularly. She seemed satisfied by the assurances, although it was probably a matter of wanting to retain the illusion.

On Monday I was a shift that overlapped with Sheena's, but not in the same section, so our breaks didn't coincide. All I could do during my breaks, when I was alone by the coffee machine for want of another non-smoker was watch her at work—which I did, as unobtrusively as possible but intently nevertheless.

I estimated that she couldn't possibly weigh more than seven stone, but she seemed more ethereal than feeble to me. The fact that her hair was black with mousy roots was only exceptional because the regular harpies mostly had hair that was blonde with mousy roots. She was still dressed entirely in black, as she had been the previous week, but a trifle more casually, in black jeans that were distinctly worn and a T-shirt whose faded legend declared, implausibly, that she was a member of the Royal Redondan Naval Reserve.

I tried to figure out some way of exchanging a few words with her, but I couldn't. If she was aware that I was watching her she didn't show it. My shift overlapped with Trudi's too, and there was a ninety-minute interval in which we were all there together, but as Trudi was also in a separate section, there was no opportunity for conversation there either, which I didn't really regret.

On Tuesday the same shift-pattern was repeated, and I began to feel that Human Resources were indulging in a deliberate exercise in frustration. Sheena was dressed in the same outfit, except that the T-shirt's legend declared that she was a member of the Israeli Defense Forces, which seemed even more bizarre. The combination qualified as dressing down even by the relaxed standards of Phoneland, but it looked good on her. I tried to watch her from my unit when she took her solitary breaks, but it wasn't easy with some idiot always burning my ears and having to maintain all the robotic protocols while wishing that he would drop dead or go to charm school.

I concluded, after long study, that Sheena did seem as if she wasn't quite there, but not because she looked as if she were mad, in spite of the slanders that Jez had reported. To me, it seemed that she was slightly faded, like a photocopy of a photocopy. Her telephone manner was exquisite, though. She spoke softly, with perfect, almost musical clarity. Unlike the members of the slag legion, she didn't give the impression of having momentarily switched off a natural and otherwise ever-present coarseness. She seemed—to me, at least—to be naturally gentle of tone and manner. She never seemed to get pissed off by the callers, which spoke of incredible fortitude, and also seemed to have a happy knack of calming them down, no matter now irate they were when they finally got past the Chopin prelude that we tortured them with while they were on hold.

"I don't think she's crazy at all," I told Jez, forthrightly, on Wednesday, when we coincided again, after completing my preliminary observations.

"Never thought she was," Jez said, a trifle inconsistently. "All that goth stuff is just posing, anyway. It's an affectation—a lifestyle fantasy way past its sell-by date. She must be about ready to get over it by now. You won't get anywhere, though. Steady boyfriend."

Apparently he was still behind the times on that one—unless Trudi was mistaken, which didn't seem likely. I didn't bother to enlighten him, but I was curious, and asked him whether he knew the boyfriend in question.

"Not to speak of," he said. "Only seen him in the distance. They were both in a shitty band at one time, but they broke up—the band, that is. I think she still does something with the boyfriend. Won't come to anything."

The theoretical option existed of asking Trudi for further information, but I wasn't about to do that. If any real opportunity had opened up to talk to Trudi I would probably have ducked it, but it didn't, so I was able to preserve my illusion of not being a coward.

On Friday, Sheena and I were on the same afternoon shift, in the same section; I'd consulted the HR rota in advance, so I knew that the opening would be there. I came to work in black Levis and a black t-shirt, whose gothic qualifications were only slightly compromised by the luminous green X-Files logo on the back, which was hidden by my jacket. I only saw her briefly in the first two breaks because she spent almost all the time in the Ladies, but eventually she came to sit on the sofa. I bit the bullet.

"As we finish at the same time today," I said, "I wondered if you'd like to go for a cup of coffee with me before we go home."

I was steeled for some kind of scornful put-off, but all she said was: "Okay." She didn't sound overly enthusiastic, but I felt free to hope that the diffidence was just a matter of being guarded and playing her cards close to her chest.

We clocked off together and made for the nearest Starbucks.

"You seem to have settled in all right," she observed. "although the girls don't seem to have invited you to join them in the Black Boar to-night."

Actually, Rachel had told me that a few of them would be meeting up, and had actually stressed the fact that Trudi wouldn't be there, because she was working the evening shift. I'd thanked for her kindness, but said that I had another engagement.

"It's probably a pleasure best taken in small doses," was what I said to Sheena.

"Have you made up your mind yet whether you want to fuck Trudi?"

"She told you about that?"

"She didn't have to. It was all over the center by eight o'clock Saturday morning."

I wondered whether the conversation I'd had with Trudi later that day had also been reported word for word all over the center, but thought that it probably hadn't. Either way, I said: "Yes."

"Yes, you've made up your mind, or yes, you want to fuck her?" Her voice was perfectly level and seemingly diffident, as if it really didn't matter to her one way or the other.

"Yes I have made up my mind, and no, I don't want to fuck her."

She arched a black-penciled eyebrow. "Why not?" she asked, innocently.

"She's not my type."

"A gorgeous blonde with blue eyes and big tits isn't your type?"

"That's my story, and I'm sticking to it—but if the entire conversation was reported to you, you already know that her opinion is that I just don't have the balls for it."

She looked me straight in the eye, and said: "I don't believe that."

I was extremely glad to hear that she didn't believe it, but I tried not to let my exultation show. "You're obviously more discriminating than she is," I remarked.

"Of course I am," she said. "Do you want to know what she said about you?"

"Well, now you've asked me the question I do, obviously."

"She says that you're too smart for your own good, though not as smart as you think you are, but that fundamentally, you're probably okay, even if you're a bit short in the ball department."

"Ouch."

"Oh, coming from Trudi, that's good. I don't think I've ever known her let a man off more lightly. You really don't want to know what she says about the ones who say they do want to fuck her…even if she eventually decides that she wants to fuck them."

"Including my brother, apparently," I said, humorlessly.

She didn't take that theme up. Instead, she said: "She says that you've been watching me like a hawk all week."

"Like I said—she has weak powers of discrimination. There's nothing hawk-like about me. I'm more akin to the Owl of Minerva."

"The one that flies only in the twilight?"

That took me slightly by surprise; I would have been prepared to bet my shirt, then, that Sheena had also heard of Messalina, and Goebbels too. I smiled. "Exactly," I said, and couldn't help adding: "You've read Hegel, then?"

"No," she said. "I read it in a story somewhere. And Trudi isn't stupid—she's probably right about you being too smart for your own good."

"True," I admitted, readily. "Why, exactly are we talking about her? There must be other topics of conversation we could try out. What about you, for instance?"

She looked away. "I've never been in here before," she observed. "The maroon plastic upholstery is seriously revolting."

"You should have seen it in the old days, before Starbucks took it over," I told her. "Before I went down south it was a seedy pub called the Cock and Crown, with a bad case of Oscar Wilde wallpaper—three pints and you wanted to fight it to the death."

She didn't laugh, but she contrived to give the impression that it wasn't because she didn't understand the joke. I took the implication from the change of subject that she was uneasy about talking about herself, but if the girls had reported the results of their findings the previous week, she had me at a considerable disadvantage, and I wanted to catch up.

"Jez told me you used to be in a band," I said.

"Yes," she said. "It split. Davy and I are hoping to do something else."

"Davy?"

"We used to be together, but we aren't any longer—not romantically, that is. It's just a music thing now."

I took due note of her use of the word *romantically*. Obviously she didn't share Trudi's contempt for such notions. "You sing?"

"And write lyrics. He does the music. We'll record a CD when we're ready."

"A DIY job?"

"That's right. It's normal, with our kind of thing."

"I know. I was never a goth, strictly speaking, but something of a fellow traveler. The Sisters were my favorite band throughout my teens."

"Good taste," she said, in a neutral tone, and swiftly changed the subject again. "If you did sociology at university, why aren't you a social worker?"

"That's social admin. If I wanted to do something like that I'd have to do a vocational qualification. I did consider the probation service once, but only for a minute. Much safer to deal with the criminal classes over the phone, and I'm too bone idle to do another year's training anyway. Where do you live?"

"With my mum, in Cross Gates. You?"

"Out past St James's and the Corporation Cemetery. No dad?"

"No. Mum was married, but I was too young to notice when it broke up. He died soon afterwards. Mum took Libby—that's my older sister—to the funeral, because she remembered him, but I didn't go. Your dad's dead too, isn't he? Cancer."

"Lungs," I said. "Caused by asbestos. He and Mum divorced before he got really sick, but he knew he had it. I don't know the whys and the wherefores. Your sister works at Gap, doesn't she?"

"How do you know?" she countered, defensively. She had to know that Trudi must have told me—but she wanted to know what else Trudi had told me, although she was too discreet to ask the question bluntly.

I dodged the issue. "Have you got any other siblings? I've got a younger sister."

She didn't complain about the sidestep. "A little brother," she said. "Lib's my full sister, but my little brother's only a half."

The conversation was flowing easily enough, but she was still wary. Figuring that platitudes weren't going to break down the barrier, I risked: "Why Sheena, out of all the names you could have chosen?"

She decided not to get annoyed by the implication that she'd once had another name. After all, I wasn't challenging the pseudonym's present reality. "I didn't choose it," she admitted. "Libby went to see the Cramps on their last British tour, shortly after I joined the scene. They had a song called *Sheena's in a Goth Gang*. Lib started calling me Sheena because she thought it was funny, in a contemptuous sort of way—it's not that she doesn't love me dearly, mind, but you know what older siblings are like. Anyway, the best way to deal with put-downs is to accept them and take them one step further, don't you think? Now I'm Sheena to everybody."

"While the real you remains secret? Why not? Does the fact that you sometimes wear an Israeli Defence Forces T-shirt mean that you're Jewish?"

"No. Davy brought it back for me from Jerusalem. He bought it in an Arab shop on the Via Dolorosa. He thought it was funny that the Arab shops were making money out of them. Maybe the Arabs did too. The Redondan Naval Reserve shirt was a present from him too. He gets the Redondan Cultural Foundation Newsletter. You'd probably like him."

I had my own ideas about the likelihood of that, but I wasn't about to spoil things by saying so. Nor was I about to ask her opinion of past life regression or vampires unless and until she introduced the topics first. A changed name is one thing; esoteric interests that she might be taking a shade too seriously were another.

"Jez says that the goth scene's changed a lot while I was away," I said, figuring that it was a safe enough observation, while heading in the right direction.

"Everything changes," she said "The Sisters are widely reckoned to be retro-goth now, but I don't necessarily agree with that. Genius doesn't age."

"True," I said. "And it doesn't care about being unfashionable. The whole point of unpopular culture is not to like the things that the majority likes, not to think the things that the majority thinks, not to want the things that the majority wants and not to do the things that the majority does. It's the only way to make progress."

She didn't accuse me of talking bullshit, for which I was duly grateful. "Of course," I went on, letting my mouth ramble now that it had got into its stride, "even an oppositional subculture has to have norms of its own. You still have to think the things that certain other people think, etcetera, etcetera. Do you want another coffee, or shall we get a drink somewhere that isn't the Black Boar?"

She hesitated for quite a long time over that one; it was probably the critical point in the relationship, which was still a closed bud with only the merest hint of a petal showing. If she wasn't interested, she could have gone home then. The fact that she didn't implied that she might be enjoying my company. I desperately wanted that to be the case.

"Okay," she said, finally. It felt like a win, because it was.

# V

We had no difficulty finding a slightly more upmarket wine bar than the Black Boar. It was 1999, after all. She protested when I asked her what she wanted that I'd paid the coffees, but I reminded her that a Yorkshireman's masculine pride is something to be defended almost as stubbornly as his wicket, and she allowed me to order her a half of Dry Blackthorn.

Eventually, she said: "What you said about the conformist nonconformity isn't really true. There's a dress code of sorts, and shared tastes in music, but that doesn't mean that we all think the same things or want the same things, etcetera. We can be as weird as we like, but we don't have to be similarly weird." She paused, and then added: "There's no such thing as being too weird, of course?" in an interrogative fashion. She was obviously familiar with Jez's opinion of her idiosyncrasies.

"Indeed not," I said, but I moved the drinks over to a table before I took my courage in both hands and said: "And exactly how weird are you?"

"Didn't the little bird tell you?"

"He made some suggestions, but obviously didn't know what he was talking about. I didn't take him seriously."

"That's because you didn't want to. You were going to ask me out, so you didn't want to believe anything too silly."

"No, honestly," I said, valiantly. "I thought it was probably bullshit, but I certainly wouldn't mind if it turned out to be true. It'd be a pity if we were all the same, as my Gran used to say.

"I bet she also used to say 'There's nowt so queer as folk,'" she suggested. "But Jez doesn't know the half of it. Do you believe in reincarnation?"

"No. Do you?"

"Yes, with complete conviction. How about vampires?" Now she was being deliberately provocative. The change of scene had obviously caused her to decide that if she was in for the penny she was in for the pound, at least to test the water to see whether a meeting of minds was possible, or whether a meeting of bodies might be possible even in the absence of an agreement to disagree about matters such as reincarnation.

I was glad, because it meant that she was seriously considering me as someone she might want to go out with again, and again after that. I knew that I had to be careful and play my cards wisely, but I didn't want to be blatantly dishonest, so as to give the appearance that I was willing to feed her any bullshit to get her into bed.

In the meantime, of course, I had to be suspicious of my own motives; even though I'd meant every word I'd said to Trudi in the Black Boar; there was a possibility, after all, that she was right, and that underneath the bullshit I really was just like all men, only out for a fuck—but I didn't think that was the case, and I certainly didn't want to think that Sheena might be another Trudi in disguise, only interested in the possibility of one night of reckless passion and one more opportunity for bile and slander. I really did have to be careful, though.

"Well," I said, carefully, "that would depend what you meant by vampires."

"Oh, right," she said. "The *anyone can drink blood if they want to* routine. That's not what I mean."

"If you mean the undead rising from their graves by night in order to find necks to bite, perennially in danger of crumbling to dust in sunlight, and invisible in mirrors, then no," I said, telling myself sternly that not only was honesty the best policy tactically, but a necessity if I wanted to lay the foundation for a serious relationship, which I was convinced that I did. I added: "It doesn't make any sense. And blood is just blood, not some magical elixir of life."

"You're right about the move version of Dracula," she said. "No sense at all. And the modernized Anne Rice version isn't much better. But there really are vampires of a sort, and you're wrong about blood. At times, in the right circumstances, it really is a magical elixir of life—and I don't just mean transfusions and bone-marrow transplants."

"And your notion of vampires is linked to your version of resurrection?" I queried, tentatively.

"Yes it is," she said, but wasn't yet ready to go into detail. She was still testing me out. And she was watching me, if not exactly like a hawk or the Owl of Minerva, in a sense that was more curious than fearful, as if she really did want to know how I would handle the question. I knew that I had to avoid being dismissive, but I also had to avoid looking as if I were simply humoring her.

"I've always had difficulty believing in anything supernatural," I told her. "It just never seemed to me to be in the slightest bit plausible. When I was a kid, Mum still went to church, and took Steve and me with her, because she wanted us to believe in God. I never could—not for an instant. Even at the age of four, it seemed to me to be an idea utterly devoid of plausibility. It even seemed impossible to me that anybody else could really believe it, and I honestly thought, and still sometimes suspect, that they were just pretending, the way they did about Santa Claus. Later, when I accepted that some people not only believe it, but somehow find it as impossible not to believe as I find it impossible to believe, I began to think that it must be a matter of the way the brain is wired, and that I just don't have the neurological capacity for belief. Maybe that ought to be reckoned an affliction, and maybe it's the capacity for belief that ought to be reckoned an affliction—I really don't know about that—but I'm a natural skeptic. That doesn't mean that I think anyone who isn't a skeptic is stupid or deluded, but it does make it difficult, maybe impossible, for me to believe things in the absence of brutal evidence."

I was scared that that might bring the curtain down, and put an end to the discussion and the fledgling relationship, but it didn't. She was interested, and also ingenious.

"Does that mean," she said, in a fashion that suggested that she too was being careful, but fundamentally honest, "that what you said to Trudi about there being more to sex than just fucking, was just empty talk?"

"No," I said, slightly surprised. "I really mean it."

"So you do believe in some things that go beyond brutal evidence? You believe in love." She didn't pronounce the word in a treacly fashion, but there was no trace of Trudi's naked contempt.

"What I said to Trudi, as I'm sure you know," I told her, "is that it might be an illusion, but that if it is, it's a necessary illusion. And I meant that, too. I'm not sure enough of my own convictions to take them as definite proof of reality. Maybe I'm being inconsistent and applying a double standard, but I honestly think that if love is an illusion, it's a necessary one, whereas God isn't, unless you want to get into linguistic games that define God as love. I'm willing to entertain the notion that God might be a necessary illusion for some people—it certainly seems that way—but it doesn't seem to be necessary for me." *Just as love doesn't seem to be a necessary illusion for Trudi*, I thought—but I didn't say it aloud, because it would have complicated the argument.

Trudi, of course, would simply have said that I was talking bullshit. Maybe I was, even though I meant every word—but Sheena was taking it seriously. "So," she said, "you'd be willing to entertain the possibility that reincarnation and vampires might be necessary illusions to some people—even that some people can't help believing in them."

"Yes."

"But you think that you're fixed forever—that you're just *wired* in such a way that you'll always find the things that you presently find implausible beyond belief, and you'll always protect the things that seem necessary to you against the skepticism of others?"

I realized that she was considerably subtler than I thought, that I'd made a mistake about the crucial point of the argument. Suddenly, I found myself out of my depth, because I really didn't know where I stood on the ground that the argument had reached.

*How did we get here?* I wondered, silently. I had to say something, though, and it was more important than ever that what I said was both true and satisfactory to Sheena.

"I'd certainly like to think that I'm more flexible than that," I said. "And the evidence surely suggests that people can and do change their convictions. Disillusionment is a common phenomenon. Conversion might be rarer, but it does happen. People yield to argument, and sometimes have what they take to be flashes of enlightenment." I paused for breath, and almost left it at that, but I felt that the whole truth was necessary, as well as nothing but. "But if you're asking me whether I'm amenable to changing my mind and believing in reincarnation and vampires, I'm not at all sure that I can. I don't want to make any false promises. Even if I tried, I doubt that I could believe in those things."

She looked at me for a long time, as if she were weighing things up. Presumably, she was. The silence can't have lasted for more than fifteen seconds or so, but it seemed like a long time. We had both finished our drinks—I'd finished my pint before she's finished her half—so neither of us was able to cover the embarrassment of the interval by taking a swig of blessed alcohol. The thought of trying to defuse the tension with a joke or a change of subject didn't even cross my mind. Looking back now, I don't think it crossed hers either, because I don't think that what she said when she broke the silence was a change of subject, and I don't think any longer that she tacked on a joke simply in order to lighten things up, although I made that assumption at the time.

"We die every night, Kirk," she said, in what might have been mistaken for her scrupulous telephone voice—although in her, as I'd already observed, even that didn't seem artificial. "We surrender our hold on consciousness, and we rise from the grave, every time we dream, hungry as well as invulnerable. We all wake up different—even those of us who never encounter a vampiric incubus or succubus. Resurrection is a commonplace experience, and so is vampirism, but most people choose to ignore them, or to reinterpret them. Our true selves are invisible to us, especially when we look in mirrors. Blood is just blood if you cut yourself accidentally, or while it's circulating routinely in your veins, but to a vampire, blood is life—and when your blood's been drunk by a vampire, you wake up different, resurrected as a new person. If it happens often enough, you can never go back to what you were before. All that stuff about shriveling up in the sunlight is complete crap, though—the movies invented that."

I burst out laughing, because I thought it the last remark was a punch-line—and when she kept a studiously straight face I still thought it was a punch-line.

"You're cheating," I suggested. "You're changing the supernatural into the merely metaphorical."

"No, I'm not," she said. "That's your interpretation, not mine. Most people don't realize how supernatural even everyday things are. Not just dreaming—all dreaming, not just the dreams that come to us in sleep—but all feeling. Life itself, even reason. It's all supernatural. Vampires are ordinary because they're supernatural, not in spite of it."

I made a mistake then. I had what I took to be a flash of enlightenment. I thought that I had cottoned on to what she was doing and why. I realized—or thought I realized—that the whole things was just an extension of the way she'd changed her name to Sheena. I thought that she was taking the put-downs and running with them, taking them so much further that all the mockery was discharged. I thought she was applying the principle that if people accuse you of being crazy, you take the bullshit on and you double it, and double it again until it becomes surreal. I thought it was cool. I liked it. I thought I could play the game. I wanted to play the game. I wanted us both to play the game.

Maybe I was a fool, but even now, I don't think so.

"I can go along with that," I told her. "On those terms, I can accept the supernatural—maybe even resurrection and vampires. If what we're dealing with is dreams and feelings, I have no shortage of those."

"That's your interpretation," she repeated, seemingly more in sorrow than in anger, "not mine."

I thought I had the measure of her, and I thought I understood the way she was playing with ideas. I really did like it. And I figured that even if I was wrong, even if I didn't have the measure of her at all, and even I didn't understand the game she was playing at all, it didn't matter. Maybe, I thought, she didn't either, and it was all illusion. If that were the case, I thought, it wouldn't make any difference to the reality of the situation, or the possibility that we could negotiate a mutually rewarding way to negotiate a way through it.

If I hadn't made the mistake—if I had known what the rules of the game really were, and what the stakes really were, would I still have wanted to play?

That, I suppose, is the million dollar question, and the real reason that I'm writing all this down, so long after the events occurred.

What's the answer?

Yes I would. I would have carried on., because even at that early point in the relationship, I was…well, I'm not going to say "hooked" again, because it gives the wrong impression, and I'm not going to say "in love," either, because that gives the wrong impression too. I was *determined*. I was committed, and not just for Trudiesque reasons. I'm not going to say that it was destiny either, or the mysterious supernatural endeavors of the vampires of Atlantis, or some kind of neurological crisis akin to an epileptic fit on the road to Damascus. It was none of those—but I was not only in for the penny and in for the pound but *all in*. My entire fortune was on the line.

Even after years of reflection I can't really explain why I was committed, or exactly what I was committed to, but there was no doubt about it. It wasn't just that Sheena was "my type"—obviously not, because she wasn't a type at all; she was unique. It was something else, something beyond any simple and glib explanation. In her terminology, it really was something supernatural—but then, in her terminology, everything was… and still is.

"So you're a vampire?" I said, trying to make it sound light without it being a put-down. "And you've had past lives?"

"Yes," she said. "Does it matter?"

"No," I said. "Not in the least. Does it matter to you that I'm not, and haven't?"

She looked me in straight in the eye, and said "I don't know yet." I guess it served me right.

I nodded my head, and said: "Sensible answer. May I take the implication that you're willing to do what's necessary to try to find out?"

She smiled then. "Do you mind if I tell Trudi about that one?"

"If you like—but she probably won't want to use it herself once she knows where it came from."

"Don't underestimate her. I told you—she's not the gorgon she makes herself out to be."

"She's gorgon enough to petrify me. Why are we talking about her again?"

"Because she's an interesting subject, and probably safer, for the time being, than my crazy ideas, now that we've settled the fact that we're going to carry on exploring them. They're best tackled gradually."

"Take it as gradually as you like," I said, "if that means I'll see more of you." It was a flat, banal line, but the situation had changed sufficiently to call for banality—which was, as she said, probably safer than further discussion of her ideas, now that we'd placed them on the agenda of the relationship in a fashion we could both deal with, in due course.

She wasn't quite ready to let the descent into banality carry us away into blissful jokiness, though. "Why me?" she asked, sounding genuinely puzzled. "If you'd played your hand sensibly, you could probably have had any of those girls you went out with last Friday—maybe even Trudi. Why put them off and single me out?"

I knew that she wasn't testing me any more. She genuinely wanted to know.

"Whatever answer I gave you would be just words," I told her. "I can't explain it, but the moment I caught sight of you, you were the one I wanted, and watching you like the Owl of Minerva has only intensified that feeling."

She nodded her head, and said, with a faint smile: "Sensible answer. Must be twilight."

In fact, it was. "It is getting late," I said. "Maybe I should take you home."

"I knew you wouldn't let me get a round in," she said, the smile broadening. "Too macho. Not exactly convincing, is it, from a sociology graduate? You should go out with the girls a few more times. That'll toughen you up."

"I'm not in the least macho," I assured her, glibly, because I'd used that particularly tactic before, more than once. "I always wanted to be, because I wanted to be like my big brother. I even took masculinity A-level, figuratively speaking, when I was at school. It turned out that I was OK on the theory but I failed the practical. One of the reasons I started studying sociology was the hope that I could learn to understand and master my inadequacies as a mere male. I could have done psychology instead, but in psychology you have to blame everything on your parents, and it didn't seem fair to Mum. In sociology, it's the entire society's fault. Share the wealth and share the blame, I say."

"Couldn't agree more," she said, still smiling. "The sins of the ultimate fathers—and ultimate mothers—visited upon countless generations. No fault at all of your Mum and mine. By the way, I forgot to ask: Do you believe in Atlantis?"

"No. Do you?"

"Absolutely. It's the key to everything. You do see what you're getting yourself into, don't you? I don't want you to have any illusions, except for the necessary ones."

I had to appreciate the ambiguity of that remark. She was stylish as well as clever. No wonder I was on the brink of falling in love.

"You'll have to spare some of my illusions, I fear," I told her. "I could maybe live without one or two, but please don't take them all. Anyway, I probably spoke too soon about Atlantis. I can believe United are going to win the league some day, and even that New Labour still intend to cut hospital waiting lists and help the pensioners, so why should I have any difficulty believing in Atlantis?"

"Which United?" she asked, in transparent jest.

"Darling," I said, "there is, by definition, only one United, whatever fools may think in Manchester, Sheffield or bloody Dundee. Did you know that Elland Road has the only five-stall dog track in the country?"

"No."

"Well then, it's obviously true what they say. You do learn something new every day. Tell you what—if you don't want to go home yet, I'll get them in and you can slip me the money under the table when nobody's looking."

"Somebody would see us out of the corner of his eye and get the wrong idea," she said. "Anyway, you're right about it getting late. I think I'll owe you one and get the last bus. You don't have to see me home. We creatures of the night can look after ourselves."

I tried to insist on seeing her home, of course, but she was stubborn—she was a Yorkshire lass, after all. It wasn't that she didn't want me to know where she lived; I think, in retrospect, that the evening had been a lot more taxing for her than she'd been prepared to let on, because she'd thought, as I did, that she was laying more than the penny and the pound on the line, and she had reached the end of her tether for the time being.

I saw her on to the bus, and gave her a peck on the cheek before she boarded, and then I walked back to Harehills Lane, alone with my thoughts, my dreams and my illusions.

All in all, I though, it was a perfectly satisfactory pre-date. Even after the brief intensity of the philosophical discussion, I didn't think Jez could be taken seriously. I didn't think Sheena was crazy. Even if it turned out that she was, I figured, and even if it turned out that I was only the kind of bastard that Trudi Hemming thought I was, I was now in a position to carry things through to the goal. But I wanted more than merely to score. I wanted much, much more. I wanted all the love I could get, and, in the immortal words of Andrew Eldritch, I wanted all the love I couldn't get, too. I wanted the Holy Grail.

I had no idea, of course, how much there actually was to get, let alone how much there was that I couldn't get, or what kind of unholy blood there was in the unholy grail, but once again, I'm absolutely certain that if I *had* known, I wouldn't have hesitated for a second.

*Carpe diem*, as Caligula might have said, and probably did.

# VI

"You want to take me ten-pin bowling at the Merrion Centre?" Sheena said, almost incredulously, when I set out my proposition for a first real date, two days after the pre-date, when Human Resources scheduled our next opportunity to share the sofa by the coffee machine.

"Why not?" I said. "Bright lights and polished lanes—the pastel pullovers are optional. We wouldn't want to go somewhere dark and gloomy where we'd fade in to the background, would we?" I'd figured that the blindside approach was best, although I'd already done what any university-educated idiot would do when faced with a tactical problem; I'd visited the Central Library and James Miles' second-hand bookshop in search of research materials.

Neither was richly stocked on reincarnation, vampires and Atlantis, but I'd obtained what I could, in the circumstances; it was 1999 and there was as yet no such thing as Wikipedia—and if anyone had told me then that there ever would be such a thing as Wikipedia, I wouldn't have believed it. It would simply have been too implausible for my hard-wired skepticism.

"Oh, all right," said Sheena, after a pause. "Anything's better than television—and I suppose, if it's good enough for Homer Simpson, it's good enough for me."

We were both on the middle-of-the day shift, so we had time to go home and make ourselves beautiful before meeting up at the Merrion. I'd decided that too safe a compromise would look wimpy, so I'd borrowed one of Steve's old black leather jackets that was still in a closet at Mum's. I already had a black silk shirt, which I'd bought under the mistaken impression that the creases wouldn't be so obvious if it didn't get ironed in an emergency, and a decent pair of black trousers. My slightly gingery hair did let the ensemble down somewhat, but I wasn't ready to start dyeing it just yet.

I half-expected Sheena to have gone the whole hog, but she hadn't. Her boots only had two-inch heels and her black leggings only had a slight sheen. Her velvety jacket was cut like a Tudor doublet with a drawstring at the waist but she hadn't done anything extravagant with her hair except for renewing the dye. Her mascara was almost conservative.

"You're not quite ready for the real me," she told me, when I told her she looked beautiful.

"I'm working on it," I assured her.

I had figured that I'd have no difficulty at all beating her on the lane. Even if she'd played before, I reasoned, she couldn't have had much practice recently, and she was bound to feel bad about having to check her boots in favor of style-disaster flatties. It turned out, however, that she was every bit as neat and meticulous with a bowling ball as she was with a phone and keyboard, and I made the mistake of starting with a heavy ball. It wasn't until I put the black one aside and accepted that I was one of nature's reds that I got into a groove. Sheena won the first game by 120–113, and I had to sweat to get the best out of three; it needed 160 to outscore her on the third and I only just managed it.

"I knew you could do it," she said, when I collected the necessary eight on a final frame spare. "You're the sort who raises his game under pressure. Not many of those about in this town. Wasted in Scott Hall Road."

"It's just a stopgap." I reminded her, reveling in the compliment as we reclaimed our footwear and gravitated towards the nearest bar that served alcohol.

"Of course it is," she said. "According to the techies, it'll only be a couple of years before the whole place disappears up its own arse. The next-generation software will let them farm the work out to people's homes. I'll have to jack it in then, mind—there's no way I'm spending all day with Mum and Marty the brat. Lib says she can get me a job at Gap, but I wouldn't want to work in a mall, and I certainly wouldn't want a job where I'd be somebody popular's crazy little sister. I got enough of that at school."

"Maybe your singing career will take off,' I suggested, as I ordered a pint and a half of Dry Blackthorn.

"I'll get these," she insisted. I let her do it; in a Mall with a bowling alley, anything goes; it's not the real world. "Davy's not ready yet," she added, as we made our way to a quiet cubicle. "He gave me a new tape last week, fresh off the sequencer, but he says it's only half-cooked. I'll find the words, but I'll probably have to change them later. He says he's a perfectionist, but he's really just a ditherer."

I wondered whether it had been a mistake to turn the conversation in that direction, but it seemed better to follow it through and kill it off rather than backtrack. "That's how you work, is it?" I said. "He does the tunes, and then you fit words to them?"

"I find the words," she repeated. "Davy finds the music, I find the words."

"Why do you put it like that?" I asked, genuinely curious. "Why pretend that it's not your own effort?"

It had always seemed to me to be a peculiar form of false modesty when writers talked about their work having a life and logic of its own, which they had no alternative but to follow, as if they were merely passive agents of fate, puppets in the hands of their own creations.

"Because that's what happens," she said. "Don't you believe in the Muses?"

This time, I was ready for any sentence beginning "Do you believe in…?" or even "Don't you believe in…?" At least, I thought I was.

"Of course I do," I said, playing the game as I saw it at that moment in time. "I'm intimately acquainted with the Muse of sociology. She wasn't one of the original nine, of course, but they had to make concessions after the publication of the Communist Manifesto or there'd have been a revolution on Olympus. Which one's yours?" I hadn't been expecting Muses, so I didn't have any names to drop; I was sufficiently grateful to have remembered that there were nine.

"In seventeenth-century France," she said, with a half-smile that I was happy to construe as a polite acknowledgement of my willing grasp of the game, "poets thought that their muses were vampiric—that they had to pay in blood for life-force for artistic inspiration. Geniuses paid so high a price that they wasted away."

I figured that it was probably another little test—another baby step in the process of her deciding whether or not it mattered whether or not I could believe in her convictions. I knew that I had to treat every such test as if it might be the crucial one that would decide exactly how close she would allow me to get, and exactly how much of her own heart and soul she was prepared to invest in the relationship.

"In nineteenth-century France," I countered, "some people thought the same about the clap—that because genius is close to madness, tertiary syphilis might be the M1 to enlightenment." I said it lightly, so that she would know that it was the kind of put-down that was laid down in order to be picked up and run to healthy absurdity.

"By that time," she said, "the art of dreaming had gone completely to pot, ruined by the easy availability of laudanum. If you know how to let yourself go when you relax or fall asleep, you don't need artificial assistance, but if you start taking a drug like that your innate supplies soon dry up, and you become addicted to the artificial substitute. As for contracting a disease in order to produce the necessary psychotropic effects, that's just ridiculous. Diseases can only produce diseased dreams. You have to attract the right kinds of night-visitors to make the connections you need. You don't have to call them Muses, but it doesn't do any harm—nor do they, even if you have to pay them a price in blood or life-force. It's all in the mind."

"That's probably why I only got a two-two," I said. "The Muse of sociology didn't come through when I needed her most. My mistake—I should have fed her better."

"It's not just blood, of course," she said. "There are other bodily fluids that will do as well—and some that definitely won't."

I got that joke immediately. "Muses never take the piss," I said.

"Neither should you," she riposted immediately, in her very best telephone manner.

I could take a hint. I thought that Sheena was letting me know, subtly, that if we were to devote ourselves to the game in earnest, I had to be careful to stay within the field of play—even if, like Elland Road dog track, it was too narrow to accommodate the sixth stall that the normal rules demanded.

"So how do you find the words," I asked, earnestly, "if you can't just make them up the way other lyricists do?"

"You lose yourself in the music," she said, with perfect seriousness. "You shut your eyes and you let it take over. It's a kind of self-hypnosis—it's not really a trance, but it *is* an altered state of consciousness. Music is a natural language, with its own meanings built in. It speaks to the emotions. It's the purest magic of all, and the greatest mystery. And if you listen—really listen—you know what it's about. A piece of music doesn't mean the same thing to everybody, of course, because our emotional profiles are so different. Music resonates in different ways in different souls. If you want to understand your own meanings—the nature of your true self—you have to find your own music, and then you have to find the words that fit it. Otherwise, you might as well be taking calls at work, reciting crap from somebody else's script."

It *was* a test, I was sure. She was probing, seeing whether I could take the argument on board—and she'd given me fair warning not to take the piss. She really did want me to follow the argument. She really did want to convince me. And she thought—surely, I figured, she *had* to think—that she had a chance of doing so. She had that much faith in her beliefs, and in herself.

I thought that the second of those items of faith was justified.

I strongly suspected that if I couldn't at least take what she was saying seriously, one way or another, it might all be off—but that she didn't want it to be off. She liked me, at least enough not to prefer loneliness, so she'd warned me as gently as she could about the dangers of taking the piss. I had to play ball. She didn't expect me to agree with her immediately, and would be suspicious if I did so that I was just humoring her, bullshitting her in order to get into her knickers. I had to be more careful, and more scrupulous, than that.

I nodded sagely, and resisted the pseudo-intellectual temptation to quote Walter Pater about all art aspiring to the condition of music. "I see what you mean," I said. "Our moods have musical reflections, and it goes much deeper than the ratio of backbeat to heartbeat. To produce the right lyrics, you need to find words that have the same emotional quality as the music. It makes sense."

"No it doesn't," she said, quietly. "It goes beyond sense, in either meaning of the term. It's supernatural."

"And it costs," I added, trying not to sound too tentative. "In blood, sweat and tears. It takes something out of you."

"It takes everything out of you," she said. "Everything that isn't just waste."

Jez's comments about the band she and her boyfriend had been in having broken up at the same time took on new significance then. The one topic you should normally steer clear of when you're trying to charm a lass into bed is her ex-boyfriend, but I already knew that Sheena wasn't subject to the normal rules of engagement. "It must be difficult," I observed, delicately, "to find the right words to fit the music of a guy you used to sleep with, but aren't any more."

"The sex was a mistake," she said. "That wasn't the way we gelled. I thought it might not matter, but it did."

Under other circumstances I might have deduced from that remark that wee Davy might have turned out to be queer, but in this particular instance I was prepared to believe that he might really be wedded to his vampire muse. In any case, that wasn't the important issue.

"We all make mistakes," I said. "I never thought it was possible for sex to be among them, but that was before I met Alison, let alone Trudi."

For all her affectations, Sheena was only human. "Who's Alison?"

"A girl I was friendly with at university. It didn't work out."

"Did you dump her or did she dump you?"

"She dumped me."

"Why? What did you do?"

"I didn't do anything. Perhaps that was the problem—too easygoing, not enough initiative, drifting along the road of least resistance. On the other hand, maybe it was doomed from the start, because we went into it with different expectations. Alison was always a practical sort of girl. She saw university as an interval in her life, something to do in order to get the qualification, and then to put behind her and get on with making use of the qualification in the real world. I think she went into the relationship with the preconceived assumption that it was something she would leave behind with the uni—something to assist her through the three years in a stable fashion, part of the educative experience. I was just one more course that she took, one more assignment she had to complete and then hand in. When the time came for her to focus all her attention on revision for the exams, she got rid of the potential distractions, including me."

"But that wasn't the way you saw things?"

"No. I wasn't methodical. I didn't have a plan, or fixed expectations. I was exploring."

"Exploring sex?"

"Exploring the spectrum of my own feelings. These things take practice."

"Yes," she said, they do. "Do you regret hooking up with such a cold-hearted bitch?"

"She wasn't cold-hearted, she wasn't a bitch, and I don't regret it. She just had a different way of proceeding in life. I'm not saying that it wasn't a nasty blow to my pride, and it certainly hurt, but it wasn't really her fault."

"Wow. It's just as well that you didn't hook up with Trudi. With an attitude like that, you'd probably have spent the rest of your life thinking that she was a really nice girl and that it was entirely your fault that she'd dumped you the next day and bad-mouthed you to all and sundry."

"Probably," I agreed, wondering how Steve felt about it. "But aren't you the one who told me that she isn't really the gorgon she makes herself out to be? I'm not the only one who finds it difficult to believe in cold-hearted bitches."

"Oh, I believe in them," she assured me. "But you have to learn to tell the real ones from the mimics. The ones who try too hard are the mimics—but for God's sake don't tell Trudi I said that."

"I won't," I assured her. "Obviously, I can't tell the difference—I tend to assume that they're all mimics. Even Messalina, although Trudi pulled me up on that one."

"You talked to Trudi about Messalina?" she said, evidently surprised. "I'm surprised she even knows who Messalina was."

"I was surprised she didn't. I dropped the name, in my usual pseudointellectual fashion, and then I had to explain."

"You explained that Messalina wasn't really a cold-hearted bitch?"

"More or less. I suggested that her reputation was all slanderous lies. She took the implication that I was making sly suggestions about her own reputation, and gave me a sharp correction. She's really quite something."

"You like her, don't you?"

"Yes, in a perverse sort of way. But I don't want to fuck her and I certainly wouldn't want my little sister to turn out like her."

"Why haven't I heard about this conversation?" she asked.

"It wasn't in public," I explained. "We were on the same break, and she dragged me outside to keep her company while she had a fag."

"Really? She must like you too, then—in a perverse sort of way, obviously. Unless she had some other reason. She didn't warn you to leave me alone, by any chance?"

I sensed dangerous ground, but it was easy to steer around. "No. She didn't mention you. She wanted to take up something I'd mentioned during the previous night's grilling. She actually seemed to have been thinking about it, weighing it up. As you say, she's deeper than she seems… deeper than she pretends to be. Not that I have an intention of exploring those particular depths. I'm avoiding girls' nights out from now on."

"You could probably get used to it,' Sheena suggested, coolly. "After the third or fourth time they'd probably go easier on you. One or other of them would probably develop a soft spot for you and let you separate her from the pack. They don't really go in for pull-a-pig contests—what's the point of playing a game it's impossible to lose? They just resent the fact that lads do, and they know it puts the fear of God into lads to think that they might be victims of that kind of contempt."

"Actually," I said, "I suspect the whole pull-a-pig mythology might be an urban legend."

"No, it's not," she said, quietly.

She was right, of course; I'd never done it myself, but I'd seen the Polaroids. I'd even laughed at them, because that was what was expected, even though they weren't at all funny.

"Well, then, all the more reason why I wouldn't want to get used to that kind of subculture," I said. "It's definitely my round this time. The next one too, obviously."

"Why obviously?"

"Because I'm drinking pints and you're only drinking halves. It's simple arithmetic."

"In that case," she said, "let's go somewhere a little less naff. We've both made our points in the bowling alley, haven't we? No need to stick to the mall."

We had, in fact, both made our points. The only places within easy walking distance where the oak beams weren't plastic and there wasn't a trace of maroon were the downmarket Upin Arms and the upmarket Countess of Cromartie. I took her to the Countess, even though I knew the harpies sometimes used it for girls' nights out. It wasn't Friday, and in any case, I figured that the risk was worth it.

"This is better," she conceded. "It has a certain antiquity, in spite of the careful gentrification."

"You'll have to show me where the Goths hang out," I told her. "I'm out of touch."

She studied me carefully. "Are you sure you're ready for that?" she asked.

"Sure. You were prepared to go to the Merrion Center; it's only fair that I make the effort too. As I said, I've always been tempted; it won't be an imposition."

"You'll have to dress the part, you know. Just wearing black isn't enough. You have to make an effort, if you're going to fit in."

"No problem," I assured her, mentally saying goodbye to my fairish hair with ginger tints, and having no difficulty at all in imagining what Mum was going to say. She would accuse me of setting Lily a bad example. Perhaps I would be, but if I had a choice between nudging Lily in the direction of Sheena and the direction of Trudi, it would be Sheena every time, even if I weren't in love with her. No lily can stay white forever, but black is always a better way to go than scarlet.

"You'll have to let me help—if you try to do it yourself, you'll muck it up completely."

"I'll be glad of the advice," I assured her.

"The girls at work will take the piss out of you. You'll probably get a derisory nickname."

"There'll be two of us, though. We might be able to start a trend— unless, of course, you don't want that, because you want to carry on being different…unique, even."

"I'd still be unique even if they all got gothed up," she informed me.

I suspected that, in her mind's eye, she was picturing Trudi as a Goth, something akin to a more aggressive version of Xena, warrior princess. I certainly was. Thinking that she probably suspected that, I hastened to add: "Yes, of course you would. You can always spot the mimics, and there wouldn't be a single real vampire among them. I presume, though, that they all have past lives, even though they don't remember them?"

"Of course."

As usual, I just couldn't help it. "Trudi might have been right, then, to correct my impression of Messalina as a slandered innocent. She might actually have been Messalina…and Cleopatra and Phryné before that: the eternal *femme fatale*"

"That's not the way reincarnation works," she told me. "And you know as well as I do that she's fundamentally okay, underneath the act, otherwise you wouldn't like her."

I wasn't sure that that was true. I had, after all, specified that my covert liking for Trudi was perverse. Cold hearted bitchiness can be attractive, at a distance. I left the point unchallenged, though. I also refrained from asking how reincarnation did work, in her view, even though the opening was there. That education was something I wanted to take slowly, just in case, when the time actually came, I couldn't swallow it. Dressing up I could do, believing six impossible things before breakfast I thought I might not be able to manage, even with the best will in the world.

"It's not going to happen anyway," I said. "If you're not a role model sufficient to inspire them, I certainly won't be. As you say, they'll just give me a nickname and take the piss."

"Do you always sell yourself that short?" she asked, obviously thinking about Alison as well as my lack of confidence in being able to provide Scott Hall Road with a goth role model.

"Pretty much," I admitted. "I like to think of it as a ploy, but it's probably just that I'm a little short in the scrotum department, like Goering."

She didn't need it explained; she knew the rhyme.

"And am I just another instance of selling yourself short?" she asked. "You targeted me because you didn't think you could aim any higher?"

"Absolutely not," I said. "And you know as well as I do that that if I'd wanted to aim low I had the entire bloody call-center laid out like a target range. I've always taken the road of least resistance in the past, but that's because I really didn't know where I was going. This time, I do, and I'm aiming for the top—the very top. The path might be steeper, but it goes in the right direction."

"And thorny," she said. "You might get scratched."

"I'll take the risk," I said, flatly. I was anticipating scratches—but not being stabbed in the heart. If I'd known…but we've already been through all that.

I would have liked to be able to assure her that she wouldn't get scratched either, that I, at least, really was the road of least resistance, one that she could walk all over in perfect security, but I didn't want to sell myself too short. Ideally, I would have liked her to believe, in fact, that I was something worth taking aim at too. I would have liked to believe it myself—but there are some things that just seem innately implausible, unless you happen to be wired the right way.

She let me buy the third round though, as well as the second, in order to flatter my image as a stubborn Yorkshireman.

Afterwards, I saw her all the way home. Sheena lived on what passes locally for the wrong side of the tracks, in Cross Gates, north of the railway and east of the ring road, but the terraced street she lived in was neatly kept—what Gran would have called respectable poor. It was obvious that Sheena wasn't about to introduce me to her mum or her big sister right away, so I left her on the doorstep after a relatively chaste kiss—but that was OK, because we'd already fixed up another date for my next day off. She had agreed to bring some of her tapes over to my place and let me cook her a meal.

Nobody had said anything about bringing an overnight bag, but it was tacitly understood that we probably liked one another well enough to make the final attempt to determined whether or not we gelled, and that if it seemed that we might, we'd cross our hearts and hope not to die....or at least cast the die and cross the ruby slipper.

# VII

I couldn't claim to be much of a cook back in those days, but in spite of my inheritance, I'd felt the pinch of student poverty sharply enough in the previous three years to appreciate how much money you can save by peeling your own potatoes and sticking your own toppings on a supermarket pizza base. For Sheena I splashed out on steaks—from the butcher's, not Tesco—and a bottle of French red. I drew the line at attempting baking, though, so I bought a couple of slices of cheesecake from the Harehills Delicatessen to serve as dessert. I'd managed to acquire three more black shirts by scouring the local charity shops, and I took the best one up to Roundhay during the afternoon so that Mum could pass the iron over it.

"Not going into the church, I presume," Mum said, perhaps a trifle regretfully.

"Ha!" Lily put in, just to let me know that she had sufficient sophistication to know what the real reason had to be. She'd just got back from school and was still in uniform, so she looked uncommonly demure.

"I'm afraid so," I told her. "I get my dog collar next week, but I'm not allowed to hear confessions until I've done the moral obstacle course."

Mum only *humph*ed, but I was proud enough of the quip to save it up to tell Sheena later.

"You really ought to get an ironing board of your own," she told me, "if you're going to start taking a proper pride in your appearance. There really isn't much skill to it—you'll pick it up in no time, and they're really not expensive. It's worth the effort. Clothes make the man, isn't that what they say?"

"No," I said, "that's hair-dye. I'm going to dye mine black, to match my outfit and my personality."

Lily was already listening, in a desultory fashion, but she pricked up her ears at that. "You're really going goth?" she queried. "I thought you didn't have the nerve." At least she hadn't said *balls*, although she probably would have if Mum hadn't been there.

"No," I riposted. "It was following Steve into the army that I didn't have the nerve for. Adapting my costume to reflect my inner self is a different matter altogether."

"Don't be silly, Kirk," said Mum. "I know your inner self better than anyone, and it isn't black. There's nothing wrong with your hair. If God had wanted it to be black...."

"He'd have given me a different set of genes," I completed for her. "But the fact he gave me yours and Dad's doesn't alter the fact that he also gave me free will, and that freedom allows me to pick my own colors."

Mum sighed. "As long as you're not going to paint the flat black too," she said. "That would be too weird."

I assured her that I had no plans to do that, even though the remark gave me pause to think that the wallpaper Dad had put up was seriously uncool, even though not up to the standard of the one that had proved to Oscar Wilde the necessity of going. I wondered, belatedly, what Sheena was going to think of it.

Perhaps Lily was telepathic, because she suddenly chipped in with: "He's got a girl. He's taken up with a goth girl." At last she hadn't said *fucking*, although she might have, if Mum hadn't been there.

"Yes I have, I said, stoutly. "And she's clever as well as beautiful. You're going to love her."

They both looked surprised at that. "You're actually going to bring her round and introduce us to her?" Mum said. "It must be serious. How long has this been going on?"

"Long enough," I told her.

"God!" said Lily. "Kirk in love! Now I've seen everything....except, I suppose, Steve in love...although...."

"Although what?" I was quick to ask. "Do you know something I don't?"

"Not really," she said, ambiguously. "Is there a woman at the place where you work called Trudi Hemming?"

My heart sank. "Yes," I said.

A horrible thought seemed to strike her then—so horrible that she didn't immediately notice that it didn't make sense. "She's not the one you're going to bring home and introduce us to, is she?"

"No."

"No, of course not," she said, catching up. "She's not a goth. It's not that Maxine, is it?"

That qualified as changing the subject, but I didn't pull her up on it; Mum's attention had been attracted.

"What this about Steve and this Trudi person?" she demanded. "I never heard of her."

Lily was my sister; sometimes, her mouth ran away just like mine did. "You must be the only person in Leeds who hasn't," she muttered.

"What's that supposed to mean?" Mum demanded.

"It doesn't mean anything," I put in. "Trudi's one of the people I work with. She mentioned when I started that she knew Steve, but only slightly. There was nothing serious between them."

I stared hard at Lily, who stared back, and said nothing.

When she went upstairs to do her homework I followed her, telling Mum that I was just going to say goodbye.

"What do you know about Steve and Trudi Hemming?" I asked her, bluntly. I hadn't got time to waste; I had to get back to Harehills and cook dinner.

"Nothing," she said. "Just that he fancied her madly, and the way she treated him really pissed him off." She was being diplomatic.

"And what did you mean about Mum being the only person in Leeds who hadn't heard of her."

"Oh, come on, Kirk," she said. "You know exactly what I mean." She looked at me with a question in mind that she didn't dare speak aloud.

"No, I haven't," I said, answering the unspoken question without any further elaboration, and added, by way of reflection: "The girl I'm seeing, and have every intention of introducing to Mum at some stage, is called Sheena."

"As in the comic book character?"

I was surprised hat she'd heard of the comic book, which was long before Mum's time, let alone hers, but guessed that she had probably seen the famously bad movie.

"Yes," I said, "but that's a coincidence."

"There are no coincidences." She was doing psychology A level as well as biology and chemistry; the syllabus included the safer bits of Freud.

"Yes there are," I said. "And for God's sake don't tell Mum that Sheena shares a name with a comic book character."

"Wouldn't dream of it," she said. "Your sex life is your own affair. Whatever weird fetishes you have, I won't be discussing them with Mum. Honestly, though—dyeing your hair black to get some goth girl into bed! It's going a bit far, don't you think? Getting Mum to iron your shirt is bad enough."

I began to foresee all kinds of problems that might arise if and when I introduced Sheena to the family. If Lily was taking that attitude now, what was she going to say when she found out that Sheena believed in vampires, reincarnation and Atlantis, not just to Mum but to Sheena?

"This is serious, Lily," I told her. "I'd really rather you didn't shoot your mouth off. I need you to be on my side. One day...."

"No chance," she retorted. "No way I'm letting you catch a glimpse of any relationship of mine. But you needn't worry. I won't say a word out of place. If it goes the same way as Steve and that slut Trudi, though...."

"It won't," I told her. "And don't go believing everything you hear about people. Ninety-nine per cent of gossip is just malicious lies."

"I was here," she said, bluntly. "You weren't."

Evidently, ego-bruised Steve had taken Lily into his confidence, young and presumed innocent as she was—or maybe he hadn't made that presumption. Tempted as I was to probe, I had to go.

"Do your homework," I told her. "I'll see you soon."

"Can't wait," she said, feigning disdain.

I thanked Mum for the ironing and headed home.

Sheena turned up fashionably late, but only by fifteen minutes. She was wearing the same mock-doublet-and-hose she'd worn at the Merrion Centre, but her boots were longer and shinier and she'd gone all out with the make-up and silver plate jewelry. Her earrings were bats and her necklace looked like something out of an ancient Saxon tomb. Her eyes looked fabulous, like pale blue suns with black holes at the core, pouring all manner of strange radiance over her lids and lashes.

She'd brought four tapes, but she told me to put them to one side until later. While I was busy in the kitchenette bring the meal to a state as close to perfection as I could contrive, she set about inspecting my bookshelves with minute care.

"Research?" she said, when I popped my head around the door to check that she was OK. She was pointing a long black fingernail at couple of paperback vampire novels I'd picked up at Miles' second-hand shop. I'd taken care to put the books on Atlantis and past life regression that I'd borrowed from the central library out of sight. A conscientious bullshitter has a duty not to reveal his sources.

"Of course," I said. "Have you read them?"

"Of course," she retorted. "I could have lent them to you if you'd asked."

"That's okay," I told her. "How rare do you want your steak?"

"Somewhere between well done and ruined."

That was a relief. She might have been a vampire, but she was a Yorkshire vampire. If she'd felt forced to conform to stereotype and eat it bloody I'd have felt obliged to do likewise, but she was obviously not a mere mimic.

A few moments later she came to the door of the kitchen carrying one of the library books, which I obviously hadn't hidden well enough. "More research?" she queried.

"That one's non-fiction," I pointed out. It was a skeptical text about the legend of Atlantis, tracking its manifestations and metamorphoses through history.

"That just means that it's dishonest lies instead of honest ones," she said. Obviously, she applied the Claud Cockburn principal instinctively—as, for that matter, did the author she was blithely slandering.

"I suspected that it might not be entirely reliable," I conceded, minimally, "although I assumed, charitably, that any errors might be mistakes rather than lies. I didn't know where to go to look for the truth unfortunately. There seem to be quite a lot of books on the subject, judging by the bibliography in that one, and they all seem to disagree with one another."

"You won't find the truth in books," she told me. "You have to find it in yourself."

"I'm not sure that my inner self has any innate information about Atlantis," I confessed.

"Of course it does," she said. "You know far more than you think you do about all sorts of things. It's just a matter of digging it out of the unconscious and bringing it into the light. It's not so hard when you know how."

"Self-hypnosis you mean?"

"Exactly. Learning to listen to music is a start. You might not get the hang of it right away, but I'll do my best to help you."

"Thanks," I said.

Two minutes later, while I was guiding the steak through well done while trying to ascertain that it didn't end up ruined, she returned to the doorway with another of the dubious treasures I'd tried to hide. That one was about memories of past lives, and was not at all skeptical. Indeed, it seemed to me to be way beyond half-baked.

"What do you think of this one?" she asked, innocently. Even an astronomer with his eyes firmly fixed on Orion wouldn't have fallen into that pitfall.

"It's interesting," I said. "I find the psychology of the remembrance quite intriguing. Unlike John Donne's poem about metempsychosis, which wonders, on logical grounds, what it might be like to remember all our past lives as insects and vegetables, it seems that the clients of spiritualist mediums can only ever remember being priestesses, princesses or courtesans. Why is that, do you think?"

"Remember that you've been warned about being too smart for your own good," she said, "not to mention taking the piss. There are perfectly sound psychological reasons for it. I'll explain them to you if you like."

"I'm sure you're right," I said, not dishonestly. "And I'll be interested to hear them. Am I to understand that if I learn to remember my past lives, I'll be restricted to human ones too—and, for that matter, male ones?"

"I certainly hope so," she said, without elaborating but somehow giving the implication that it wasn't an entirely casual remark.

"I guess I get the better part of the deal," I said. "History being what it was, the most comfortable incarnations have usually been male—except perhaps for the really remote ones, back in the days when the Mother Goddess was supposedly all-powerful."

"Yes indeed," she said, her voice becoming lighter again, to emphasize the humor. "Being a dryad in Arcadia was okay—satyrs put merely human males in the shade, equipment-wise—but being an Amazon was even better. I liked the lives I led in Atlantis best, though."

I moved the steaks on to the plates, after holding one up so that she could give it a nod of approval, and added the vegetables, checking as I went so that she could control the quantity.

"Where, exactly was Atlantis?" I asked her. "Thera, in the Med, or north of the Azores?"

"In the Atlantic," she told me, but further west and further south than the Azores."

"Somewhere around the mid-Atlantic ridge?" I continued, as I carried the plates through. I'd already opened the wine an hour in advance to let it breathe, so all I had to do was pour it.

"Don't try to pretend that you know more than you do about vulcanism and the mid-Atlantic ridge," she advised me, as she carved a chunk off her steak. "I can read too, and construct an argument, and it would all be a colossal waste of time."

"Fair enough," I said. "Were you joking about satyrs and nymphs in Arcadia?"

"No," she said, simply.

"It must have been painful amputating your left breast so that you could use a bow when you were an Amazon there," I observed. "I hope it didn't get infected."

"Oh, we had anesthetics and antibiotics in Arcadia,' she said. 'It wasn't until the Dark Ages that the last remnants of traditional female learning were wiped out by male doctors. Don't knock it—you'd love getting in touch with an Amazon self, if you could. Think of all that lesbian sex!"

"But I can't?" I said. "Males only, right?"

"I'm not saying it's impossible," she said. "It's just not the way it usually works out. There are questions of affinity involved. I don't know about the Donne thing you mentioned, but I suspect that getting in touch with an insect or a vegetable would be even harder."

"There wouldn't be any direct line of descent there," I said, pensively, "so there couldn't be any race memory."

"That's not how it works," she told me. "You don't have to be a direct descendant of the people whose past lives you can access. As I said, it's a question of affinities."

"And you have affinities with nymphs and Amazons?"

"Apparently. But only fleeting glimpses. Atlantis is the real heart of the matter, the key to everything, at least so far as I'm concerned. That's where my prime template is."

"You mean was?"

"No, is. All times still coexist. In a sense, Atlantis is still my present, and this life is just a kind of reflection."

I couldn't help remembering the impression I'd had, when I began to study her seriously, that she was somehow reminiscent of a repeated photocopy, slightly fainter than a real person ought to be. I no longer had that impression, Now, if anything, she seemed to me to the only real person in my surroundings, and everyone else had become slightly blurred and out of phase. Apparently, though, she had a sense herself of being some kind of copy—of an original in Atlantis.

*It could have been worse*, I couldn't help thinking. *If the original had been a one-breasted lesbian Amazon.... Except, of course, that I don't have the full story on the Atlantean vampires yet. But if that's the original to which I'm magnetically drawn, by destiny, lust or some kind of affinity, what does it say about me, psychologically? If she wants to put me in touch with my prime template, what am I going to be, in her imaginative estimation? What do I want to be? Not a satyr in Arcadia, I dare say, but what are the alternatives?*

Chewing had deflected us from talking for a little while, but I was beginning to feel that the silence was dragging a little.

"You're going to teach me to do the self-hypnosis thing, right?" I said.

"If you like," she said, as if I really had a choice, although I knew that I didn't, if I wanted to take the relationship further forward. At some stage, obviously, I was either going to discover what my unconscious was going to throw up under the power of her suggestion, or at least summon up something from my own imagination under the same power of suggestion. It would be the same thing, really: the same Muse, the same poetic product...and the same cost.

"Not that I expect too much, of course," I said, letting my mouth ramble on, only weakly connected to my train of thought. "I realize that finding out that I'd been Napoleon—or even Max Weber—would be the equivalent of winning the lottery on a rollover week. With my luck, I'd probably turn out to have been a eunuch in a Caliph's harem."

"I made contact with of those once," she told me, serenely. "Great singing voice—that was probably why I leapt the sex barrier for once. Every incarnation leaves its mark, but some are more welcome than others."

She might well have been joking. I realized that from now on, she could tell me anything, and I wouldn't be able to tell whether she was joking.

"On the other hand," I said, speculatively, "maybe it would spoil my enjoyment of the present slightly to be always comparing it with the edited highlights of half a dozen or a thousand lifetimes. Don't you find that?"

"It's actually the other way about," she countered, presumably having met the argument before. "The only way to get a true appreciation of what it means to be alive—or undead, if you prefer to put it that way—is to have died a thousand times. Until you've lived a million long-lost joyful moments, you can't properly realize how precious they are. Anyway, once you've had a glimpse of other worlds, this one can never be enough. If you don't learn to dream advantageously, you're letting most of life's potential go to waste."

"Does the soul have any choice about its incarnations?' I asked, realizing as I did so that my pretended curiosity, improvised to keep the conversation going, was fundamentally genuine, and not artificial at all. "Does it simply get assigned to the baby whose birth coincides most closely with the extinction of the previous incumbent, or can it hang about and wait for a better opportunity?"

"It doesn't work like that," she said, again. "The notion that there's a soul that enters your body before birth like helium in a balloon, and exits again when the body-balloon pops or deflates, is oversimplified. There's a sense in which there's only one soul, of which our conscious selves are just ever-mutating fragments, which can sometimes make contact with one another and communicate, reflecting or establishing a fundamental identity of individuality: unity amid multiplicity, and multiplicity amid unity."

"Oh," I said—and tried to work out some logical consequences of that way of thinking, although I knew that I'd need hours, and maybe days, in less distracting circumstances, really to begin to get to grips with it.

I cleared away the plates while I was thinking, brought the cheese-cake slices and topped up the wine-glasses. Then I sat down again and studied her. She was so beautiful I wanted to pick her up and carry her into the bedroom there and then, but I knew that a certain amount of decorum was called for, and that patience would serve to enhance the quality of the eventual release.

"You said reflecting *or establishing*," I repeated. "Does that mean that you have a measure of control over the connections that you make with your past lives."

"In practice, not very much, although I think one can get better by working at it—the more closely you're in touch with the sequence of your past lives the more control you obtain,' she assured me. "It probably works both ways, though, and most of the control that's exercised on present incarnations probably originates in the past."

"Possession, you mean?" I said, slightly alarmed.

"That's a bad term," she said. "Haunting is better. Some ghosts are just personalities that get stuck, and recur passively, like echoes, but others seem to be exercising a precious skill. Vampires tend to be experts at hanging around—it makes it easier to visit sleepers and take their blood. If necessary, you can get right inside the beating heart, bathing in the oxygen-rich flood from the pulmonary vein. In some ways, though, shed blood is better, especially if it's offered freely, as a kind of libation."

I thought she might mean the pulmonary artery, but unlike Lily, I'd dropped biology at thirteen, so I knew that I could be wrong, and even if I wasn't, it didn't seem, any longer, to be the kind of conversation in which an abrupt dose of pedantry would be appropriate or welcome.

"Forgive me if I'm being stupid," I said, instead, "but are you saying now that vampires aren't physical beings at all, but more like ghosts: parasitic haunters, reaching out of the past to draw life from the blood of the present?"

"No, we're not parasites," she said. "That's very crude thinking. The blood we draw isn't vulgar nourishment, like this cheesecake. It's like the symbolism of blood-brotherhood. The mingling of the blood helps to create, or strengthen, the connection between different fragments of the universal soul, helping to reflect or establish the affinity, the identity."

I wasn't keeping up. I knew that I'd need a lot of time to think about it, and probably a lot more instruction from someone who knew—or thought she knew—what she was talking about."

"Does that mean, then," I said, cautiously, "that you won't actually be wanting to suck my blood?"

"Of course I will," she said, as if were the most natural thing in the world. "There's no rush, but eventually, it will be necessary. Is that a problem?"

"No," I said.

"That's what I thought. "It doesn't hurt much, and it's only a matter of a few drops—far less than the hospital takes from blood donors."

"Right," I said. "Symbolic. A libation."

"If the prospect turns you off," she said, "we don't have to go that far. I'm not making it a condition. I've decided that I'll sleep with you anyway. But it won't be….what I'm really looking for."

"There's no problem," I repeated. "I'd like you to find what you're looking for, if it's possible. I'd like to find what I'm looking for, if it's possible…although I'm not at all sure that drinking blood is going to help….even yours."

"Trust me," she said, "it will."

I believed her.

Why did I believe her? I don't know. I don't know myself well enough, even now, to analyze it. Maybe it was just the fact that I was literally aching to spend the night with her, maybe it was just the fervor of that desire, the psychotropic effect of that lust, that was frying my brain and putting me in a state of mind where I'd have believe anything at all, at least for that night, at least until I woke up the next morning. Perhaps the fact that the imprint it left lasted a lot longer than that was just a neurological accident, a forged connection of neurones laying down an arbitrary pathway.

But I don't think so.

I can't deny the possibility. I have no defense against the cynical argument, but even so, I don't accept it. There was a different kind of affinity involved, something beyond mere lust…and even "mere" lust, remember, in Sheena's way of thinking, was something supernatural, something with a music of its own. I believe, still, that there was a connection between us, an affinity between us, that added a measure of symbolism to the notion to sharing blood that was far more than any simple sexual fetishism.

# VIII

From that moment on, I really did want her to find what she was looking for, eventually. And I wanted to find what I was looking for, once I'd figured out what it was. But I also wanted to lighten the mood, because sometimes, things can get too intense.

"I'm not sure I'd like to discover in my past lives that I'd been Vlad the Impaler or Caligula," I said. "It seems to me that there are risks in this regression business."

"Of course there are," she said. "There are risks in everything. But as for those particular worries, they're highly unlikely, given the enormous odds. Statistically speaking as you pointed out, you'd be far more likely to find that you'd been a eunuch." She grinned, perhaps to reassure me that that remark, at least, was just a joke—but I was far from sure.

"Or a satyr, if accounts of Arcadia can be trusted," I suggested, dryly.

"Actually, no," she said. "Satyrs were never very common, and they were very long-lived, whereas eunuchs...."

I remembered too late what Winston Churchill had said about statistics.

"I'm teasing," she said, obviously having figured out that I couldn't tell any more. "I told you that you shouldn't keep selling yourself short. Do you really think I'd have been attracted to you if you were the latest manifestation of a sequence of eunuchs, or impalers, or mad incestuous emperors? I've been around in the rich tapestry of eternity, remember. I know quality when I see it."

I wasn't sure that she wasn't still teasing, but it did make a kind of sense. The attraction between us had obviously been mutual, if a trifle tentative on her part to begin with. Given what she believed, she had to think that it meant something, that there was more to me than met the eye, and far more than some random plonker with a mediocre degree in sociology and a pleasant telephone manner.

"Thanks," I said. "And I know you told me not to sell myself short, but I can't help feeling that if you're hoping to find the reincarnation of Hercules or Orpheus, you might have come to the wrong shop."

"They weren't all they were cracked up to be," she assured me. "History exaggerates."

"So who would you like me to be?"

"I can't tell you that," she said. "If I told you, you'd be attempted to construct—or, far worse, pretend. You'll have to find out who you were for yourself, with the aid of music and memory."

That, I realized was going to be the ultimate test, the ultimate guessing game—and I was going to have to play it in the dark, with no light to guide me, unless I could worm the clues out of her slowly and slyly.

"I see," I said. "And what if it turns out that I've never been a vampire in my past lives? Would that make a difference to you...to us?"

"You're fishing," she observed. "Don't. And don't jump to conclusions, either. When the time comes, just let it come. Just open the vault of the unconscious, and see what emerges. You might be surprised."

That was what I was afraid of. I would far rather have known what to expect, or at least what to hope for.

"But you remember being a vampire yourself?" I queried thinking that it had to be a fair question. Your...prime template was a vampire?"

"Yes. Once you've been a vampire, you never forget it, although the memory remains buried in the unconscious even of most of the vampire's affiliates. Of all the things that make their mark, vampire identity is one the most powerful. It's not quite once a vampire, always a vampire, but there's a definite predilection."

"Like a curse, handed down...well, not from generation to generation, apparently, but from...affiliate to affiliate? A transtemporal sisterhood."

"Some might think it a curse. Some have, In fact."

"But not you?"

"Of course not."

I reminded myself of Jez's judgment that it was all just a show, just an exotic lifestyle fantasy, and I told myself that I ought not to forget that, that I mustn't get sucked in too far, no matter how fascinating the game became or how satisfying the carnal rewards. But I also reminded myself that all lifestyle is fantasy, and that there's no virtue in buying a mass-produced lifestyle off the peg in Gap, or anywhere else, if you have the wherewithal to design and make your own, especially if you can do it in the erotic context of a *folie à deux*.

Did I believe any of it? No, I didn't, not really—but the more important question was, did it matter? Did I believe anything at all? I was prepared to believe that Joseph Goebbels had existed, but not a single word he'd ever said, or, given that he'd apparently had lots of children, the allegation that he had no balls. I believed that Messalina had existed too, but not that anything ever written about her lack of morals was true.

The important thing about all the unorthodox information that Sheena was telling me was not whether it might be true, or even whether it could possibly be coherent, in some abstract philosophical sense, but whether she believed it, and whether or made sense to her. If I was prepared to accept the fake history that historians invented, in order to make political sense of the world, and the autobiographies that people distorted, in order to fit in with it and justify themselves, why shouldn't I be prepared to accept the fake history and fake autobiography that Sheena had invented to make psychological sense of herself and justify herself within that context?

So, although it would be a lie to say that I never asked myself the question of whether any of it could really be true, in an objective sense, it certainly didn't seem, at any stage, to be a question of any real relevance. If it were, in fact, all just a matter of playing a game, well, as Bill Shankly reportedly said about football: "Some people think it's a matter of life and death, but it's really much more important than that." If my going along with what Sheena told me about herself, and what Sheena asked me to do for her, was playing a game, picking up a metaphorical ball and dribbling it, it was a game that was at least as important to me as life and death, and I was prepared to give it my full attention, with deadly earnest.

We had long since finished the cheesecake, but we had a little of the wine left, so we were able to carry our half-full glasses to the couch. It was difficult to tell how mellow Sheena was, because her veiled eyes and meticulous pronunciation didn't give much away, but I saw the tension in her limbs as she went to put on one of the tapes that she'd brought to play me, and I realized that I wasn't the only one who was putting myself through a series of tests in order to win approval. She was nervous about the tape. I was about to hear her singing, and singing her own lyrics. That was one aspect of her being on which I hadn't yet judged her, and she felt that there was a risk. She was scared that I might not like her singing, and her words, and she wanted me to like them.

I wanted to like them too, but I had a shrewd suspicion that I wasn't going to be able to fake it convincingly if it turned out that I didn't. If I couldn't relate to the music, and her role within the music, no amount of bluster and empty flattery would be enough to cover it up. She was too smart, and too sensitive; she'd know. Although she still didn't know that much about the real me, I felt sure that she already knew enough to see right through me in that one vital respect.

I didn't really know what to expect, but if I'd had to guess in advance I'd probably have opined that heartbreaker Davy's music would tend to the gloomy, the ethereal and the tuneless. Sheena's remark about seventeenth-century French poets and their vampiric muses had left me with an impression of her relationship with Davy, and although I'd never read a word of seventeenth-century French poetry in my life, I simply assumed that it was dark, nebulous and leaden.

I was dead wrong, about twentieth-century Leeds if not about seventeenth-century Paris. These days, with fancy keyboards, synthesizers and samplers, drum machines and computer software, one guy can pretend to be a whole ensemble, or even an orchestra. Davy didn't seem to want to be an orchestra, but he didn't want to be some morose bastard sitting in the dark with a mournful acoustic guitar either. The backing track on the tape was multi-layered, replete with insistent percussion, but by no means unmelodious. It was dark and strange, but there was nothing in the least effete about it. If anything, it was a trifle too full-blooded for my pop-educated taste.

Sheena was so softly spoken, and so seemingly fragile, that I'd expected her voice to be thin, maybe tending towards falsetto or whispery, but it wasn't. The register was lower than I'd anticipated but the notes were well rounded, not in the least hoarse. If her lyrics had been written out as if they were prose or blank verse they might well have looked clumsy, maybe even meaningless, but I could see right away what she meant about finding meaning implicit in the music and choosing words to echo and amplify it.

I knew that I wouldn't be able to follow or remember the convolutions of the lyrics until I'd heard them at least half a dozen times, but certain phrases and repetitive refrains immediately stuck in my head. The dark romanticism of the music was reflected in images of night and death, but there was a lot more that obviously derived from Sheena's fascination with remote and probably imaginary pasts. There were no explicit references to Atlantis or Amazons, although vampires featured in some tracks—there was even one called *Graveyard Love*—but the half-whimsical conversation in which we'd touched on those subjects allowed me to catch references I might otherwise have missed—to the extent that I began to wonder whether I'd really been as much in charge of its subject matter as I'd thought.

When Sheena sang about falling stars or the wings of time or the loneliness of castaways she wasn't simply redistributing the standard pick-and-mix materials of teenage angst. I knew that I'd have to go a lot deeper into her fantasies if I were to get to the bottom of her lyrics, and that I'd have to put some work into solving the mysteries with which they'd been liberally salted. Because I had other things on my mind— well, one other thing on my mind—I didn't really make much effort to listen with full concentration, and might not have been able to lend more than half an ear to the tapes as she ran through them with dogged persistence, too embarrassed to offer much in the way of commentary. That half-ear was, however, sincerely appreciative, and some of the couplets penetrated deeply enough to recur long after the tapes had run through.

"I like that," I said, of one refrain, which ran: "To kiss and sting through some emergent world/Reeking and dank from out of the slime."

For the first time that evening, she blushed.

"It's Byron," she admitted. "I borrow, sometimes."

If there were more misappropriations, I didn't pick them out, and I certainly didn't recognize any sources—but I probably wouldn't have. One that seemed to me to be more than likely to be hers, though, was: "I need to be free, of myself, of myself/ I need to be free, of myself."

I hadn't a clue what it was supposed to mean, but it seemed to me to be heartfelt.

First impressions don't always cut deepest, but if they stick, they stick hard, and Sheena must have known that before she selected the order in which she played the tapes. The couplets that wormed its way into my consciousness most avidly, and stuck most securely were on the earliest tracks she played. There were other neat refrains, but the one I seized upon as if it were a key was *I want to be free, of myself.* It didn't sound, in Sheena's voice, like a mere artifact or affectation. It sounded intensely personal, as it presumably was, given her fascination with past lives and her conviction that she was only a fragment of some larger, time-spanning personality. What was perhaps more surprising was that it somehow found a resonance in me that the more fanciful imagery didn't.

Davy's compositions weren't the kind of music you'd ever hear on *Top of the Pops*—which still existed back in 1999—and I wasn't sure that they were the kind of alternative that John Peel would ever have championed before he turned into a comedy teddy bear and died, but they certainly weren't amateurish or inept. By the time the second tape clicked off, I had relaxed, no longer afraid that I was going to blow my chances with Sheena by being unable to take that aspect of her seriously—and when she saw me relax, she relaxed too. She'd remained standing after putting the third tape on, but after three or four minutes of tape four she sat down.

"I could have brought some earlier stuff as well," she said, 'but this is more or less where we're up to now. Davy says it's not right yet. It's partly the mix, he says, but bits of it need rethinking. When he's got the fundamentals right, he says, I'll be able to find the right words." She was rambling slightly, becoming nervous again. Before she'd played the music, she'd been focused on that as the next hurdle to overcome, but now the music was finishing, there was another in view.

"It's good," I said, by way of a summary opinion. "It works. It's distinctive, and it works—which is good."

"Would you like to meet him? Davy, I mean."

I hadn't been in any doubt as to her meaning, but I wasn't sure what the right answer was.

"Not tonight, obviously," she added, swiftly. "Sunday, maybe, if you're not doing a late shift."

"Would he want to meet me?" I asked. I didn't want to be paraded before an ex-boyfriend as some kind of trophy, displayed in order to make him think again about the wisdom of casting her aside like a worn-out sock—if that was what had happened; it wasn't a topic we'd explored in any detail yet.

"He wouldn't be jealous," she assured me, having recovered enough of her composure to read my hesitation. "He really wouldn't mind—and it would help you to understand." She didn't specify whether she meant the music, or her, or both.

"Sure," I said. "Sunday. Why not? It's not as if I'll be in church—still have to pass the moral obstacle course, as I told Mum this afternoon."

After I'd explained the reference in a little more detail, she said, "You've been hearing my confessions."

"Yes," I said, "but you don't need absolution—and if you did, eating my cooking is penance enough for anyone."

"It was good," she said, perhaps a trifle belatedly. "I'm impressed."

"Can't go wrong with meat," I said. "Stick it under the grill till it turns brown."

"It only seems easy," she assured me. "The accumulated unconscious wisdom of a thousand unremembered lifetimes. Who knows? Back in the Stone Age, you might have been the caveman who first came up with the idea of cooking." I didn't need a hint to know that that was a joke.

"I think it was earlier than that," I said. "I seem to remember being an *Australopithecus* at the time. Weren't you the woman who came up with the idea of cutting up gazelle-skins to make clothes? I thought we'd met before."

I wondered briefly what the United strikers could have been doing since the days of Mitochondrial Eve to have so completely mastered the art of kicking a ball the size of a dead man's head into a rectangular goal. I drank the last of my wine and reminded myself that there was no hurry at all. Within her lifestyle fantasy, Sheena and I had already had all the time in the world, and we could take that legacy to bed with us when the time came, even though I couldn't remember a single damn thing that had happened before 1984—by which time I'd already been more than five years undead for what still seemed to me to be the one and only time.

"Did you really like my singing?" she asked, still not quite willing to trust her judgment on that issue.

"Absolutely," I assured her. "I love your voice. It's like everything else about you."

"You haven't tested everything else yet," she said, half to herself, thinking about the hurdle still to come.

"I'll love that too," I assured her. "Trust me. There's no possible doubt."

There was, of course, plenty of doubt in my mind as to whether she was going to love that part of me, but I certainly wasn't going to voice it. According to Ecclesiastes there's a time to live and a time to die, and although he didn't say so in so many words, there's also a time to shut up and get on with it. But he was wrong, for once, about all being vanity and vexation of spirit. There was nothing vain about that night, and no vexation of spirit whatsoever.

Mercifully, Dad, possibly in a spirit of optimism but more probably because it happened to be cheap, had equipped the bedroom in his belated bachelor pad with a double bed, so we weren't unduly cramped, as Alison and I had been when we first had it off in a Hall of Residence. We were able to luxuriate, and luxuriate I did. And how.

# IX

Actually, the last couple of paragraphs might contain a hint of exaggeration, not of how I felt about it, but of the mundane reality of the event. The sex was by no means terrible, which is really pretty good, for a first time with someone new, but neither of us had had enough practice to be anywhere near perfect, and we were both anxious. It felt comfortable, though, and it felt right, which was also good, for a first time. Not that it was ordinary, of course, and not just because looking down at those fantasized eyes was almost as strange as looking up at them. No first time can ever be ordinary, because it's all exploration. Maybe there'll come a day when I've experienced all the different shapes, sizes and textures that women come in, but I can't believe that, any more than I can believe that in the course of a thousand associated lifetimes I've already done it.

There's no point in my trying to describe how Sheena's body felt, because even if I had anything to liken it to, I'd have no way of knowing whether anyone else could understand the likenesses—and in a way, I'd prefer to believe that nobody could. She was slim and silky, firm and flowing, but none of those words really signifies anything, because they're all mere measuring devices, which only operate in a world of common sense and common sensibility. Even the kind of perfunctory and dismissive sex that the harpies presumably went in for after bouts of binge drinking can't entirely be reduced to that. Sheena would have said that even that was supernatural, and that sex with her was much farther out, but she would have been speaking metaphorically, at least about the harpies.

We both knew, I assume, that it could have been a lot smoother and more relaxed, and undoubtedly would be in future, but I think we both took comfort from the awareness that it was really pretty good, for a first time. In fact, if I were honest enough to put the caution of hindsight aside, as well as the temptation of hyperbole, and try to recall how I actually felt at the time, it was far better than pretty good.

We'd only had the one bottle of wine between us, so there was plenty of margin left for further intoxication. We went at it hard enough to exhaust ourselves, and if we hadn't been on such tenterhooks we'd probably have fallen straight into Dreamland. In fact, we were too uneasy to release one another from our mutual embrace in order to relax into sleep, and just uneasy enough to play one more round of the collusion game.

"You didn't bite," I observed, neither wonderingly nor accusatively.

"I didn't have to," she said. She didn't mean that she'd had her fill of other bodily fluids; the vital ones were safely contained in a twentieth-century French letter. She meant something subtler.

"No," I agreed, "you didn't. Not for that. But if you're going to be my Muse...."

"I think I am," she said. "I wasn't quite sure, until now, but now I am. You can mention it, by the way. You don't have to pretend you didn't see them."

I knew what she meant, just as she knew that I knew. We'd kept the bedside light on. I'd seen the scars beneath her breasts, thin and not very long, but multiple. I hadn't been planning to mention them, because I really didn't want to know who had inflicted them, and who had drunk the droplets of blood that had oozed therefrom. The thought that really troubled me was the idea that I might be expected to inflict more. Suffering cuts was one thing; inflicting them....

The bedside light was still on. She could see my expression.

"It was me," she said. "And it was some time ago. The doctor called it self-harming, and practically threw a hysterical fit insisting on how dangerous it was. I didn't think of it as harm. It was interesting. Sometimes, it didn't bleed at all, and sometimes, it bled a lot. I never could figure out why. But I really wasn't trying to hurt myself, and it wasn't a sex thing. Davy never cut me. He refused, and wouldn't let me cut him. And if and when you want to share my blood, you won't have to cut me either, if you don't want to. That's not what it's about. It's not an S&M thing."

"I don't understand," I said.

"I know," she said. "But I think you will. In time, I really think you will."

"Am I going to have to cut myself?" I asked.

"You can if you want," she said. "I can do it, if you prefer."

I was no longer hyped up by unslaked lust. If anything, I had a touch of post-coital triste. I was having doubts. She could see that.

"It doesn't matter," she murmured, very softly. "It doesn't matter, if you can't. It's not a condition. If that's not what you want me for, it's all right. Even if what we just did was just one more notch on your bedhead, it's all right. If that's all you need from me, it's all right."

"It's not," I said. "I want more. You can have my blood. It's yours, if that's what it takes. I just don't understand why."

"You will. Give me time, and trust me. You will—but if this goes on, even if it's only what we just did, you'll be changed forever. I don't need to bite to draw blood, or even to use a razor blade. If you give me enough chances, I'll get right into the chambers of your heart and change you forever. I'm not just a vampire, I'm a special kind of vampire."

As the monologue went, on the musical quality of her voice was enhanced, as if she were fitting her words to secret music—or finding her sentiments in some melody that only she could hear. The way we were entangled allowed me to feel the heartbeat behind her ribs—and I knew, even though I couldn't hear the secret music, that it had a greater surge and power than anyone would have realized who was only conscious of her slenderness and physical frailty.

"A lamia?" I suggested.

"A lamia's a snake-woman," she whispered. "I'm not a snake. Human through and through. A dozen or a thousand times over, but always a human vampire. No curse at all, just a lust for blood and every clever way to take it in. It won't kill you, but it will change you forever. You'll have make up your mind whether you want it or not. There's still time to back out, or limit it to this."

I wanted it. I was in love, and not just with her fragile flesh. She was too weird for Jez and everyone like him, but she wasn't too weird for me. The best way to defuse a put-down is to pick it up and run with it, until you've transformed it into a way to fly, and I decided that I was with her a hundred per cent when she said that there was no such thing as too weird in our world.

I wanted the sex, again and again and again, but I wanted more. I wanted to be changed forever. It only takes one psychotherapist to change a light bulb, but the light bulb has to want to be changed. I wanted to be changed. I wanted to shine, as brightly and as darkly as her paradoxical eyes. I had glimpsed new possibilities, and I wanted them actualized.

If you fall asleep in that kind of mood, you can hardly be surprised if you dream. So I did, and I wasn't.

In my dream, I looked at myself in a mirror and couldn't see myself. I asked Mum if she could see me in the mirror, and she couldn't, but she merely told me, in that no-nonsense Yorkshire way of hers, that it didn't matter, because she could see me in the flesh, so why would she ever feel the need to look at me in a mirror? I knew she was right, in the dream, but I wasn't sure that it was as simple as that, even though I used an electric razor and didn't need to see myself in order to shave. Perhaps Mum would need to see me in a mirror, I thought, if I became a gorgon when I changed, with snakes for hair and a gaze that could petrify people.

Afterwards, in the dream, I did become a gorgon, and it was *wicked*. I went around petrifying people deliberately, and it gave me a real thrill to do it. Mercifully, Sheena—who was, of course, undead—wasn't affected by my baleful gaze, so we could still get together and wander through the frozen world like two playful demons, mocking the comical Polaroids that everyone else had become, lads and lasses alike. It was as if all the people in the world had become victims of our lust. Their clothes weren't petrified, though, and the mobile phones in their pockets kept going off, like the phones that escaped the Paddington train wreck unscathed, as the distant loved ones of the dead tried to find out what had happened to them. All the stupid customized ringing-tones formed a crazy symphony that had far too much percussion in it to be plausible, and the beat went on and on and on until the only way to stop it was to wake up, and ease myself slowly away from Sheena's sleeping body.

I woke up, but she didn't. She was sleeping very deeply indeed, as if her spirit really had fled her undead body in order to go wandering through space and time, as a blood-sucking succubus. She really couldn't bite anyone if she was insubstantial, but I knew now that she didn't have to. She didn't even have to suck semen into her cunt, or lick the tears from grief-stricken eyes. For her, vampirism wasn't a matter of sinking pints the way lads sup ale. It was authentically supernatural. She could leech the blood out of a man's veins, the marrow out of his bones, the elixir of life out of his very soul, with the most delicate touch of her purple-stained lips, or maybe just the hypnotic gaze of her neutron-star eyes.

*I can do this*, I said to myself, not quite aloud. It was the most joyful discovery I had made in twenty-one years, five months and twenty-two days, or maybe in a thousand lifetimes. I felt like the missing link who'd invented cooking, or a newborn skeptic unexpectedly risen as a vampire from the coffin where he'd fully expected to rot. I didn't just think I could do it—I knew.

It's like that, being in love; your powers of apprehension become supernatural.

I believed in the supernatural, at that moment. At least, I half-believed—which is fair enough, given that when I'd told myself "I can do this," without the slightest shadow of a doubt, I was really only half-right.

It wasn't until we got out of bed the next morning that I saw the bruises on her thighs.

"Jesus Christ!" I said. "Did I do that?"

"I guess so," she said. "Don't worry about it. It comes and it goes. Sometimes I bruise really easily, other times hardly at all. No sense to it. It's the same as the scars—and even worse with my periods—one month it's red Niagara, the next it's almost a no-show. The pregnancy scares I had with Davy…well, I soon learned not to worry too much. My legs get bad sometimes, and I have to live on aspirin for days. Had to go to casualty a couple of times—but it's okay. I'm not as fragile as everyone seems to think I am. Trust me."

I knew that she hadn't put in the comment about the pregnancy scares just to remind me that she had a real history as well as a thousand imaginary ones. She was preparing the ground for a lasting relationship, because she was sure now that I really did want in. If I'd been a United player, I'd have been over the moon or extremely chuffed, but as a con- scientious avoider of cheap footballing clichés, I was content to be very, very pleased indeed.

Sheena was on an afternoon shift, so she had plenty of time to go home and change. I started at nine, so I had to get a move on. Jez and Trudi had started even earlier, doing the early morning shift, but they were in different sections, so I didn't see them at any scheduled breaks— except that Jez hung around after his shift had ended, sitting on the sofa drinking coffee, waiting for my next break to come along.

"As soon as I joined him, he said: "I hear you slipped the ferret to the Queen of the Jungle last night!"

I was genuinely amazed, but I struggled hard not to show it.

"Who told you that?" I asked, finally, my eyes automatically flicking in the direction of the seat that Trudi was no longer sitting in, having left when her shift ended.

"It's gone round the center like a dose of the flu," he informed me. "No other topic of conversation in fag alley, so I hear. Come on, mate, you know how things work around here. Everybody knew you were cooking dinner for her last night, and everyone could follow the logic of it. Nobody had to check to see whether she's gone home afterwards. Don't worry—I'm not about to ask you for a blow-by-blow description, and nor is anybody else…but being lasses, they are going to ask her for a full report on you. I thought I'd better warn you. You're going to be a topic of conversation for at least two days. After that, it'll all be forgot- ten, but don't be surprised if remarks are made in the interim."

"By Trudi?"

"Not necessarily. As I say, just stick it out. It won't do you any harm. Maybe the reverse. Nobody else hereabouts has ever got into her knick- ers, and more than a couple have tried."

"I don't want a reputation," I said.

"Too late, mate," he said. "This time tomorrow, you'll have one. But don't worry. If I'm any judge, Sheena's not the kind to run you down, the way some would."

I didn't think that Jez was much of a judge, generally speaking, but on that particular point I thought that he was dead right. Sheena wasn't going to run me down. It wasn't her style.

I managed to attract her attention when she arrived for her shift, and beckoned her over to my unit before she clocked in. She seemed surprised, as if she were worried that I might be advertising our relationship, but she came. I put my hand over the receiver just long enough to mouth: "Everybody knows," with a pained expression.

She just shrugged her shoulders. She didn't seem at all perturbed. She knew how things worked in the center. She had anticipated that everyone would know, later if not sooner, and the fact that the inference had been drawn instantaneously didn't astonish her or upset her. She simply went to work—but when her first break time rolled round and she disappeared, as she often did, she wasn't alone in the Ladies; the other two girls in her section followed her in, and didn't come out again. I knew that it wasn't because they were so desperate for a pee that they had completely forgotten to have their usual fag.

Before I clocked off I drifted past her unit. She was on the phone, inevitably, but she mouthed: "It's okay. Don't worry."

We had already agreed to meet up when her shift finished, so there was no need to say anything more.

I left, still feeling a trifle unnerved about the fact that my sex life had suddenly become everybody's favorite topic of conversation—and that slight nausea became something much worse when I found Trudi Hemming standing in Scott Hall Road, waiting for me.

"You and I need to have a talk," she said, linking arms with me as if I were one of the members of her coven.

I didn't move. "What about?" I said.

"This and that," she said. She didn't let go of my arm, but the pressure she put on was relatively gentle. "Come on, then. I'm not going to bite."

That might have been a perfectly harmless casual remark, but it didn't seem so to me. Nevertheless, I allowed myself to be drawn away without actually being dragged.

Somewhat to my surprise, she didn't head for the Black Boar, but only took me to Starbucks.

I let her buy me a double espresso; I figured I might need it, and I was afraid of a stinging remark if I asked for a latte. She ordered the same for herself. We didn't sit in the same booth that was hallowed in my memory as the site of my first pre-date with Sheena, but in an opposite corner.

"Don't look like a frightened rabbit," she instructed me. "I told you I'm not going to bite. We're friends as well as colleagues now, aren't we? We can have a friendly cup of coffee together."

I pulled myself together. "Of course we can," I said. "What do you want to talk about?"

"Three things," she said. "First of all, I wanted to tell you that you were right about Messalina."

That was a bolt from the blue, completely unexpected. All I contrived to say was: "What?"

"Messalina," she repeated. "Wife of the Emperor Claudius, remember. *Carpe diem*—which I now know means *seize the day*, no thanks to you. I went to the library and looked it all up. And you were right. It is all lies—about Messalina, not *carpe diem*."

"How do you know?" I asked, genuinely intrigued.

"Well, I didn't just assume, like you did. I worked it out. There are two parts to the story, and they don't fit. At least one of them has to be false. On the one hand, there's all that crap about her working secretly in a brothel under an assumed name and holding sex competitions with professional whores, and on the other hand, there's the story about her marrying her lover while her husband was out of town, and getting herself executed for treason in consequence. Now, it's obvious, at least to a woman, that if she was the kind of woman who'd do the first, then she wasn't the kind of woman who'd do the second, and vice versa. As the second is more likely to have left historical traces than the first, that's the one that's more likely to be true, if either of them is. Either way, the first story is a load of crap. You were right, she was slandered. I still say that's not necessarily to her credit, but I know that you think so, so thought I ought to let you know. Okay?"

I was so busy trying to follow the subtext of what she might be trying to imply about herself, that I let my mouth make the error of saying; "Very kind of you."

"I'm not telling you to be *kind*," she hissed. "I'm being *honest*."

"Sorry," I said, reflexively.

"That's okay," she said. "Now, about your sister...."

That made me sit bolt upright. "What!" I said, in a very different tone of voice.

"Don't get your knickers in a twist," she said. "Still not biting—or being kind. Just a point of information. I take it you don't know that while you were wining and dining Sheena last night, she was phoning round all of her friends asking for all the information she could get on your new girl-friend?"

"No," I said, bewildered. "How do you know?"

"Acquaintances in common—and the fact that she wasn't just asking her friends what they knew, she was asking them to phone other people who might have information. Within an hour she had a whole grapevine set up. Amazing. I don't know about you, but I didn't have a mobile phone when I was seventeen, I never thought then that I'd be a dinosaur before I turned twenty-one, but things change so fast nowadays. Kids her age live in a different world. God, I sound old. Anyway, you know what they say about six degrees of separation. It didn't take long for the goss to start feeding back to her—but it was a two-way process. You know what I mean?"

I could follow the argument, but not well enough to get ahead of it. I didn't say a word, and had to hope that I looked more like the Incredible Hulk in a bad mood than a frightened rabbit.

"Well, what I mean is that the news that she was asking around got back to Libby Howell in no time at all, and Libby rang me, partly because she thinks I'm keeping an eye on Sheena at the center and partly because my name had come up in the conversations that your little Shanghai Lily was having all over town."

"Your name? I repeated. "Why?" As soon as I'd said it, though I guessed.

"She's somehow got it into her head that I broke your brother's heart, and she doesn't want the same thing to happen to you, apparently. She's obviously got the wrong end of more than one stick, and I figured that you might want to know, in case you wanted to set her right about a few things—Sheena, obviously, and maybe her big brother too."

"Oh," I said. It had obviously been a really bad idea for Steve to cry on Lily's shoulder, when the poor kid can't have been more than fifteen.

"You know, obviously," Trudi went on, "that I screwed Steve once, some time ago, but you must know, too, that I didn't *break his heart*. Bruised his ego, maybe, but I didn't say anything about him that I haven't said about dozens of other blokes. Anyway, he knew what he was getting into. He didn't have any illusions. I'm not apologizing for it, and I really don't mind your little sister putting it about that I'm a cross between the Empress Messalina of Leeds and the Scarlet Woman of the Apocalypse, because it can only help the image. Also, I'm the last person in the world to want to give anyone lessons in discretion—but I thought that you might, as she seems to be linking Sheena's name with mine, at least in her suspicions. And you have some idea, don't you, what impression the information that she collected so avidly will have given her?"

"Oh, shit," I whispered. I really couldn't think of anything else to say. I wished that I hadn't mentioned Sheena's name when the little pest needled me about it—but how could I possibly have known that she was going to launch a full-scale investigation, coupled with her reactions to whatever Steve had blubbered all over her when the stupid pillock had vented in her direction?

Then another thought struck me.

"Hang on," I said. "Why did you call her *Shanghai* Lily?"

She looked at me hard, as she didn't know exactly what question I was asking. She deduced the truth. "Well, well," she said. "A reference that the smartarse doesn't know. That's two-one...not that I expect to get the best of five. It's an old movie. Never seen it myself, but Marlene Dietrich has a famous line in it. You really don't know what it is?"

"No," I admitted.

"Well," she said, "the line is: 'It took more than one man to change my name to Shanghai Lily.'"

I must have gone white. If I'd been able to turn into the Incredible Hulk, obviously, I'd have gone green, but as things were, it was a toss-up between white and scarlet. I didn't say a word, but I probably stared at her as if she really was Medusa.

Oddly enough, she softened her expression. "I said I wasn't going to bite, didn't I?" she said. "I hadn't realized that one would penetrate so deep. If it's any consolation, it's not what her friends at school are calling her, so far as I know. It's a really old movie. I made the name up just now, and I won't repeat it. And for all I know, her score might still stand at zero. Okay? Are we friends again now?"

I took a deep breath, and managed to regain control, but I didn't say that we were friends any more than she had apologized for petrifying me momentarily.

"Anyway," Trudi continued, "that's your business. I just thought, as a friend, that I ought to let you know. The way I'd planned it, it was supposed to bring us on to the third question smoothly and neatly—I hadn't anticipated the interruption."

I knew that the third thing had to be Sheena. "It's none of your business," I said.

"Absolutely none," she agreed. "I'm not going to ask you any rude questions, although I imagine that Sheena's getting the third degree as we speak...except one. I suggested to you once before that you might want to be careful, because she's in a vulnerable place, but you didn't know then what I meant. By now, you probably do. In fact, I'm not even going to ask you to give me an answer to the question, but I am going to ask you to ask yourself. Now that you know, more or less, what you're getting yourself into, can you do it? Others have tried, and let her down. It's not that I care, you understand, but I know that you do. So you need to ask yourself, before you take it any further, whether you can really do it—because, believe it or not, she's not the only one who stands to get hurt."

She was lying, of course. Plainly, she did care. I could even understand why. As a career bitch, she'd carefully excised the sentimental segment from her own soul, but she hadn't been able to discard it entirely, It was still parceled up inside her, and she still felt an affinity of sorts for that part of Sheena, whom she saw as a kind of negative counterpart of herself.

Or maybe not; you know me by now: bullshit by the yard for any occasion. It was, in any case, irrelevant.

I didn't know how much Trudi really knew about Sheena's supposed secrets, but I expected that I could find out from Lily, as soon as I'd finished telling her off, whatever was common knowledge. I had to assume that she knew enough, as well as being careful not to give anything away.

"I can do it," I said, flatly.

"I'm not just talking about dyeing your hair and dressing up."

"I know. I can do it."

Perhaps surprisingly, she nodded. "I thought you could," she said, as if she had some reason to be satisfied with the result.

"Why?" I said.

"Why what?"

"Why did you think I could do it, when others have tried and let her down, given that you think I'm too smart for my own good and a bit short in the ball department?"

That was probably indiscreet, since Sheena had specifically told me not to tell Trudi she'd said that, and although I hadn't, in to many words, Trudi was bound to guess, but the gorgon didn't seem in the least annoyed. Indeed, she actually smiled.

"Not quite smart enough, then, are you?" she said. "Think about it. If you can't work it out, ask me again next time we have coffee, and I'll explain it. Just know that if the going gets tough, I have confidence in you—and if you need someone to talk to, for God's sake don't blub to your little sister. I've got to go now, and doubtless you have places to go and people to see, but I'm glad we had this little chat."

With that, she got up and headed for the door, leaving me sitting in the booth. I was a trifle slow following her, but she'd stopped outside the door to light a cigarette and I nearly caught her up—but she hardly spared me a glance as she resumed walking, and I paused again in order to give her a start.

Perhaps perversely, I was glad we'd had the "little chat" too, even if it had been one more ordeal to add to the list. What I wasn't glad about was the fact that I ran into Jez, Rachel and one of the other girls from the center as I was making my way to the bus stop, and realized that they must have seen Trudi and me coming out of Starbucks, albeit at a distance, and must have realized that we'd been together even though we'd hardly looked at one another while making our exit.

Inside the center, a certain discretion had been compulsory, but outside, the personality change induced by the phones was completely switched off. Jez, moved by a sentiment of male solidarity, merely nodded in a matey fashion, but Rachel, apparently feeling compelled to play red-lipped monster, immediately weighed in with: "Come on, then, Kirk, show us yer love bites!" and cackled, while her friend said: "Don't worry, we won't tell Sheena that you're already sneaking around with Trudi"—meaning that she intended to report to the entire call center staff at the first possible opportunity that I'd been seen having coffee with the Scarlet Woman of the Apocalypse less than twenty-four hours after "slipping the ferret to the Queen of the Jungle."

Jez looked embarrassed, and took me aside.

"Sorry about that, mate," he said. "They don't mean anything by it."

The two harpies allowed him to move out of eavesdropping range, but they were obviously waiting for him. The thought occurred to me that the day's gossip might have stirred up ever-latent erotic urges.

"Are you going out with the girls?" I asked.

"A few of us are meeting for a drink," he said, trying to keep a straight face.

"Well, bully for you," I said. "If I run across you in the Headrow stark-naked and handcuffed to a lamp post in the early hours, I'll call you a locksmith—but don't expect me to lend you my coat."

Then I caught the bus out to Easterly, intending to have a stern word with Lily as soon as she got home from school, and before I went to met Sheena.

# X

There was no way in the world that the grapevine could have got any information back to Mum, but the fact that she'd ironed my shirt would have given her enough of a clue to save her from needing any uncanny powers of divination even if Lily hadn't forced a more specific admission out of me.

"Did you have a nice time last night?" Mum asked me, blandly.

"Lovely," I assured her.

"It's serious, then?"

"Very."

"Well, make sure you clean the lavvy regularly," she advised. "Strong bleach, mind—and buy a new brush. Keep the Hoover busy, and buy an ironing board. Just peeling your own potatoes won't impress her for long—lasses expect more than that nowadays. And whatever else you do, don't get her pregnant."

"That's okay," I said. "She's a vampire. Vampires don't get pregnant."

"They do if you don't use protection, love," she said, with a sigh. "Believe me—I know."

Mercifully, Lily arrived home before the conversation had a chance to become even more embarrassing than that. I didn't waste any time whipping her upstairs to "do her homework."

"What in the name of heaven do you think you're playing at?" I asked her.

She looked genuinely startled. "What do you mean?" she asked.

"Phones work both ways," I told her. "It didn't occur to you that last night's little inquisition was going to start alarm bells ringing all over the city?"

Evidently, it hadn't. She blushed. "You mean Sheena knows I was asking about her?"

"If she doesn't, she's practically the only person in Leeds who doesn't. And what possessed you to couple her name with Trudi Hemming's?"

She decided to be defiant. "Well, why shouldn't I?" she said. "They work together, don't they? And they've both seduced one of my brothers, haven't they? Why wouldn't they look like two peas in a pod to me?"

"Well, for one thing," I retorted, "because you've never clapped eyes on either of them, or you'd know that they were more like chalk and cheese. And for another, you haven't a clue what you're talking about. I don't know what kind of *femme fatale* image of Trudi Steve managed to give you while he was sounding off about her hurting his feelings, but believe me, he knew what he was getting himself into, and he has no one but himself to blame."

Sometimes, you can't fight fire with fire without increasing the temperature. Her defiance stepped up an order of magnitude.

"And do you know what you're getting yourself into?" she flung at me.

"Yes I do," I retorted. "A hell of a lot better than you do, at any rate. And if you think I'm the hapless victim of some scheming woman, you couldn't be more wrong. Sheena's no more a *femme fatale* than you're Shanghai Lily."

That one just slipped out, thoughtlessly, but it stung much harder than I'd have expected. "Where did you hear that?" she demanded, weakly, having suddenly lost all the wind from her sails. Evidently, more people had seen the old movie than might have been expected, or had at least heard the line quoted. And even if Trudi really had made it up spontaneously, just for my benefit, she obviously hadn't been the first to do so.

"You're just going to have to get used to it, kiddo," I told her. "Blame Mum for saddling you with the name."

"Oh, I do," she said. "It's bad enough naming your daughter after a flower that symbolizes purity, without the additional insult of rhyming with silly. And it's no picnic, believe me, to find that once people stop calling you Silly Lily they're going to start calling you after some whore—but I didn't expect it from my brother."

"Sorry," I said.

"And what business is it of yours how many men I might or might not have had?"

"That's a bit rich," I pointed out, "since you seem to consider to very much your business how many women Steve and I might or might not have had."

Then she burst into tears, Frankly, I'd much preferred the defiance.

"Pardon me, for caring," she said, between sobs. "I just wanted to know whether you were going to get yourself hurt."

It was probably only half a lie, and she certainly wasn't going to admit that her principal motive had been lewd curiosity, so I figured that the polite and diplomatic thing to do was to take her at her word.

"And what would you have done about it if you'd found out that I was in danger?"

"I'd have tried to help," she said, with a naivety that might have been touching if she'd been younger, but sounded suspiciously like Silly Lily at seventeen.

"That's kind of you," I said, confident that she wasn't going to react to the suggestion like Trudi, "but it's not helpful. The hares you started running stirred things up a bit. I don't know whether Sheena knows, and I don't suppose she'll mind much if she finds out, but her elder sister seems to have taken offense at the prying, and she knows Trudi. I know it's a big city, but we all live in a relatively small part of it, and our social circles overlap. You have to be careful. Gossip spreads like an epidemic, but much faster, and it can be a veritable plague. I don't care what people say about me, but I do care what they say about Sheena."

A hint of the defiance came back. "You should," she said.

"What's that supposed to mean?"

"Don't you want to know what I found out? What I got back from the innocent questions you wish I hadn't asked?" Now the defiance was flooding back. At least the tears had dried up.

I was tempted to say no, but it wouldn't have been honest. Trudi obviously knew something about the dangers of dating Sheena, although I had no way to estimate how much, but Trudi had an inside track, and was evidently more discreet than her image suggested. I was, in fact, quite curious to know what the grapevine had to say about the object of my adoration.

"I suppose you'd better tell me, so that I can set you right." I said, fencing cleverly. "You'll be meeting her soon enough, and I don't want you going into that with any misconceptions."

"Believe me, I won't be," she said. "It's common knowledge that she cuts herself. Not that uncommon, apparently. She's anorexic, thinks she's lived past lives and drinks blood. She's seriously crazy, Kirk. Do you really want to be involved with someone like that?"

"Yes I do," I said, bluntly. "And the gossip has got it all wrong, or at least twisted out of all recognition. For a start, I watched her eat a steak and cheesecake last night, and I can give you a hundred per cent guarantee that she isn't anorexic. She's only thin because she's had health problems in the past. She did cut herself at one time—not that uncommon among teenagers today, as you say—but she doesn't any more. I've seen the scars, and they're old. She does believe in past lives, but that's not that uncommon either, and not evidence of craziness just because you don't believe it. I've talked to her about it, and she's obviously put a lot of thought into her way of looking at the issue. She doesn't drink blood, but in the days when she was cutting herself she did rationalize it as a kind of offering, akin to rituals of blood-brotherhood that are very common, anthropologically speaking, and whose symbolism is almost universally recognized. There's nothing in the least crazy about it."

"No?" she countered, skeptically. "Does that mean that you're going to cut yourself too, and mix your blood with hers, *symbolically*?"

"It might, if that's what it takes to get close to her," I said. "At any rate, I'm going to learn to hypnotize myself, to see whether I can remember any past lives. Is that okay with you, little sister?"

"Would it matter if it wasn't?"

"Of course it would—but it wouldn't stop me."

"And you're actually considering cutting yourself, just because you want to get into her knickers?"

I forgave her the vulgarity; it could have been worse.

"No, Lily, that's not what I meant by getting close. It goes way beyond that. I'm serious about this—very serious. It's not crazy, and it's not because I've been seduced; I had to work hard, believe me, to get to where I am now, and I really don't want the relationship to be torpedoed by something silly. That's why I'm talking to you."

"Well, don't come crying to me if it all goes tits up."

"Is that the way you and your friends talk nowadays?" I asked, being deliberately naïve.

"Of course not," she said. "We're much cruder when there aren't any adults around." She didn't mean it as a compliment that she was including me in the adult category.

"Well," I said, "just because you put everything into crude terms, it doesn't mean they really are crude. Just because you always say fuck, it doesn't mean that there's no such thing as making love, and calling your vagina a cunt doesn't make it filthy."

If she was shocked by my using that terminology in her presence, she didn't show it.

"I know that," she retorted. "I'm not stupid. And just because Kirk rhymes with berk, it wouldn't necessarily make you any more of one than being Lily makes me silly, or a virgin, but in this instance...."

"Berk is Cockney slang," I told her. "It has no business in Yorkshire. Likewise jerk, which is American. We're not in Scotland either, so it doesn't necessarily retain its religious connotations, but I don't care— I'm sermonizing anyway. I do care what you think of me, Lily, and of Sheena, and of me-and-Sheena. I'd like you to be on my side, and that means trying to see things to my point of view. It means not prying, and most of all, it means not spreading slander. Can you do that for me, please? As a favor?" I had slipped into my telephone voice, calm and soothing.

"Well," she said, after a pause, "since you put it like that…okay. As long as it makes you happy."

I kissed her on the forehead, and then I headed back to the flat, in order to tidy up. I hadn't had time to do anything before going to work, and Mum's admonitions had pricked my conscience slightly. I still had more than an hour in hand before I went to meet Sheena, and I intended to spend the bulk of it straightening the place up after our night of orgiastic feasting and passion.

Mercifully, I did have time to make a start on that before the doorbell rang. It was a woman I didn't know, who looked to be about the same age as me. She had bleached blonde hair but she was too well dressed and neatly polished to be placed in the same category as the slags at work.

"I'm Elizabeth Howell," she said. "Mr. Markham, I presume?"

It took a full five seconds for the penny to drop; I had never taken the trouble to work out what "Libby" must be short for. When it did, reflex made me say, "Sheena's not here. She's at work."

"I know," she said. "Can I come in for a minute?"

I opened the door wide and stood aside to let her go past. By the time I'd closed it and turned around again she had already begun her scrupulous examination of the premises. She made not the slightest attempt to cover up the fact that that was what she was doing. She took in my furniture, my bookshelves, my CD collection and my PC in a single hawk-like sweep before turning her critical eyes on me. I tried to meet the critical eyes squarely, taking note of the fact that although they were blue, they were much darker than Sheena's. Libby was taller than her sister, although not as tall as Trudi Hemming, and rather voluptuous. No one, seeing her and Sheena together, would have jumped to the conclusion that they were sisters, but they weren't quite chalk and cheese; there was a ghostly facial similarity, a hint of affinity.

"Aren't you going to offer me a cup of tea?" he asked. "Don't worry, I won't keep you. I know when you're meeting Sheena. I'll even give you a lift, if you like."

In fact, the idea of offering her a cup of tea hadn't even crossed my mind, but I took the hint. While I put the kettle on and dropped two tea-bags into mugs she continued her tour of inspection. I was glad that I'd cleared the table, and profoundly glad that she didn't go into the bedroom to sniff the sheets.

She had sat down by the time I carried the mugs into the living room, and seemed to feel quite at home.

"Tru says you're all right,' she observed.

"Tru?' I queried. Again the penny was ridiculously slow to drop. She meant Trudi, obviously.

"Wasn't as obliging as our Suzy," she admitted. "Wouldn't take the nickname on—but I keep trying. Don't like to fail."

"Trudi told you I was all right?" I said, slightly surprised, even though I knew that she'd used the phrase before. I also knew that Libby, like Sheena, must know that, coming from Trudi, the compliment wasn't as lukewarm as it sounded.

"Says you'll probably be good for her. Don't know about that, myself. She's head-over-heels. Never good to be that dependent. If you're mucking her about, you know…."

"You'll do terrible things to me," I finished for her. "That's okay. I'm not mucking her about. Didn't Trudi also tell you that I don't have the balls for that?"

"She did mention your other assets," Libby agreed. "She says that you think you know it all, but that you're really as innocent as a babe in arms."

"Do thank her for me," I said. "That's probably the best reference I've ever had. Did she also tell you that she's already had a word in my ear about…last night?" I meant Lily telephoning round; it didn't occur to me until the words were out of my mouth that she might think I meant the orgy of feasting and passion.

In fact, though, she picked up the correct implication. "I'm not worried about your sister asking questions," she said. "It's what sisters do. I'm not worried about what she might have heard either, because I assume that you'll put her straight, if you haven't already, so far as you can."

I didn't have to say: "So what are you worried about?" I knew that. I picked up on the more important point. "So far as I can?" I repeated, with an emphatic interrogation point.

"You don't know everything," Libby told me.

"And you came here to tell me the rest?" I queried, with a hint of irritation.

"No," she said. "Not yet. I will, when the time's right. Until then…."

The irritation was growing. "Don't muck her about. Believe me, Miss Howell—or can I call you Libby?—I'm not about to do that."

"Call me what you like," she said. "Just assure me that Tru's got it right and that you're hoping to be good for Suzy." She was staring at me, trying to give the impression that she had a built-in lie detector.

"Sheena" I corrected, automatically. "Her name is Sheena." I let her take the assurances for granted. She'd already checked me out with her gimlet eyes as best she could, and she wouldn't necessarily have believed anything I said to back up what Trudi had already told her. I was a man, after all, only after one thing, by definition…except that even Trudi seemed prepared, in this instance, to make a partial exception for me.

"The reason I came round," she said, without pressing the point, "is that Mum  asked me to call. She'd like you to come to dinner on Saturday. It's only fair, as you've fed Sheena." She emphasized the name slightly, to demonstrate that she's taken my correction aboard.

"Does Sheena know you're asking?" I asked.

"No. Mum knew that there was no point asking her to ask you. That's why she asked me. Once you've accepted, you can tell Sheena, and she won't be able to avoid it, will she? She won't mind, I assure you. She'll probably be quite glad. It's just that…well, sometimes, with Su… Sheena, you have to take a slightly roundabout approach. You'll find that out, if you haven't already."

I hesitated, asking myself what Sheena would want me to do, and not getting a clear sight of the answer.

"Mum's keen," Libby added. "It's her wedding anniversary. She likes to have a family meal. If I had a boyfriend, I'd bring him too, but I'm between at present."

"Wedding anniversary?" I echoed, confused. "I thought…."

"Is there any law that says a widow can't celebrate her wedding anniversary with her daughters?" Elizabeth Howell demanded. It would have been anything but safe to enquire, even in jest, whether Mrs. Howell also celebrated the anniversary of her husband's death, or the anniversary of her son's conception. I suspected that the anniversary was just an excuse, although I couldn't quite figure out what it was that Libby and her mother were excusing.

"All right," I said. "I'll have to check with Sheena, obviously, but if it's all right with her, it's fine by me."

"Seven-thirty," Libby said, in a friendlier tone, now that she knew that I wasn't about to make any difficulties. "Maybe you are all right. Our Suzy certainly thinks so."

"Sheena," I corrected, reflexively.

"Oh, all right," she said, with a fake sigh. "Sheena. I don't see why I should have to keep it up. Since I started it, I ought to be entitled to call it off, but if it's what she wants… but do me a favor, and don't correct Mum when she calls her Suzy. Are you going to join the goth gang too, dye your hair and wear the wristbands? It won't suit you, you know."

"If Sheena thinks it will suit me," I told her, "the hair will be black before Saturday, and whatever kind of show she wants me to put on for your mother, I will."

Libby shrugged. "Probably the right answer," she conceded, grudgingly. "And don't worry—she'll probably ask you to tone it down for Saturday and be on your very best behavior. She's only human, whatever she might think."

She looked at me sharply, seeking evidence of a reaction. I didn't even blink. I stood up. "Well, I'm glad to have met you," I said. "Thanks for calling. Shall I give your regards to Sheena?"

"Sure," she said. "Do you want that lift into town?"

"No," I said. "I've got some more housework to do first."

She looked at her watch, plainly aware that I wouldn't have the time to do anything useful, but she didn't try to insist. She stood up, and let me escort her to the door.

"See you Saturday, then," she said.

"God willing," I agreed. "And Sheena, of course. Not necessarily in that order of priority."

She condescended to smile.

I relayed the entire conversation to Sheena, virtually word for word, when I met her from work and we went into Starbucks for a coffee. We sat in our booth, not the corner to which Trudi had taken me, but I did feel a slight twinge of guilt.

"They're just trying to be friendly," she assured me. "It's just an excuse to make a big show. It'll be hell, but it's best to go through it and get it out of the way. Hopefully, your family will be more diplomatic and let you decide when you want to submit me to their inspection."

"Yes," I said. "About that...."

"What, already?"

"No, no...but I thought I'd better warn you, if you haven't already heard it from someone else, that I mentioned your name at home yesterday, while Mum was ironing my shirt, and my little sister took it into her head to start ringing round all her friends and asking them what they knew about you."

"Ah," she said, frowning. "And what did they think they know about me?"

"It doesn't matter," I said. "As soon as Trudi told me, I went straight home, and I put her straight."

Sheena was still frowning. "Trudi told you?"

"Yes. News of Lily's investigation reached Libby, Libby told Trudi, and Trudi told me. She grabbed me after work and dragged me in here, so that it would be private, but Rachel and Jez saw us leaving, albeit separately, so if anyone makes snide suggestions to you about me meeting Trudi behind your back, that's what they mean. She wouldn't thank me for saying so, but she was just being kind."

"Was she?" said Sheena, in an even tone, laden with skepticism—but then she corrected herself. "Yes, I suppose she was. No wonder she didn't want anyone to know about it. Look, I'm sorry that too many people are poking their noses in. God knows why they all think it's any of their business…but it'll all die down next week. And we don't care, do we?"

"Of course we don't care," I told her. "We're young and in love. We don't care about anything in the universe but looking into one another's eyes." I said it lightly, but I was looking into her eyes, perhaps a trifle too earnestly.

She blushed, and looked down. "You hardly know me," she said. "And since you won't tell me what it is you had put your sister straight about, it must have been…well, less than complimentary."

"That depends," I said. "When Lady Caroline Lamb said that Lord Byron was mad, bad and dangerous to know, she didn't mean it as a compliment, but it added a whole order of magnitude to his charisma."

"Is that what people say about me?" she asked, perhaps more sharply than she intended. "Mad, bad and dangerous to know?" Considering that she was prepared to plagiarize Byron in her lyrics, she didn't seem as grateful as she might have been for the comparison. Maybe Byron hadn't been entirely flattered at the time, even though he had probably deserved it, given that the rumors about his versatile sex life probably weren't all mere slanders.

"No," I said, "I was just using that as an example."

She thought about it for a moment or two, and the said: "It's probably true, though."

"You're not mad," I told her, "And you're certainly not bad. As for dangerous to know, well, that's not altogether a bad thing, is it? Life can be very bland without danger. Not that you'll ever be able to compete with Trudi, on that score—but that's not necessarily a bad thing either, is it?"

"You don't really know me," she reminded me, pensively. "And… well, sometimes I think it would be a lot better to be like Trudi than the way I am."

"Not from my point of view, it wouldn't," I assured her. "I think I could forgive you almost anything, but not that. And I do think I know you well enough to want to know you even better, and for a long time."

"I should hope so," she said. "But I don't really know you, do I? I don't know how deep the bullshit runs. And no matter what Trudi might have said to Libby, she knows even less about you. When she says that you think you're a lot smarter than you really are, that's just the kettle calling the pot black—but for God's sake don't tell her I said so."

"Nobody knows anybody, really," I said. "Everybody knows that sincerity is the key to successful acting, and that if you can fake that, you're made, so everybody tries, and those of us who really are sincere look just like all the mimics. But I think you really are sincere, and I know I am, so when you say *trust me*, I do, and I'd like to think that when I say, *trust me*, you will too."

"That's a good line," she said. "Remember it—it might stand you in good stead when I've been committed to the loony bin for my own protection."

I took hold of her hands and squeezed them.

"Trust me," I said.

She sighed, smiled wryly, and said: "I do."

# XI

Having consulted Sheena on the subject, I decided not to dye my hair before the weekend, so that I could present myself in Cross Gates for dinner on Saturday looking like my old self rather than my projected future self. She felt that her mother might feel more comfortable with that. I found when I turned up, after hanging around in the next street for five minutes to make sure that I wouldn't be early, that she had followed a similar policy herself. Although dressed in black, she was wearing a neat blouse and skirt, with no jewelry at all and very moderate eye-liner. I was wearing an ordinary long-sleeved black shirt and black chinos, so we were well-matched, in tasteful contrast with Libby's scarlet top and her mother's pale blue blouse.

Mrs. Howell was no taller than her younger daughter, and considerably shorter than Libby, but she was much stouter. She had probably been pretty thirty years before, but she hadn't aged well, perhaps because she was so nervous, indecisive and fluttery that she gave the impression of having been hyped up on her own adrenaline practically all her life. I did my best to put her at her ease, but there was nothing I could do to make the slightest inroads into her innate anxiety.

The meal wasn't exactly hell, although it was certainly a bit of an ordeal for everyone, even Libby. As purgatories went, though it could probably be reckoned reasonably successful. No mention was made of the supposed anniversary, which had presumably served its purpose in providing an excuse for the invitation. The food was average and the canned lager Mrs. Howell had thoughtfully but mistakenly laid in for me was drinkable in spite of the gas. I probably put one too many away while Libby and Sheena shared a six-pack of Strongbow.

Little brother Martin had obviously been instructed to talk to me about football but he felt that his duty had been done once we had exchanged a few ritualistic utterances about the leakiness of the United defense away from home and the falsity of the assumption that a four-all draw at Everton counted as "value-for-money entertainment" when all that really mattered was bagging the three points. Libby was friendly enough, although her relentless campaign to win Sheena away from Phoneland by extolling the virtues of Gap as a go-ahead retail operation poised for great things in the twenty-first century became a trifle tedious once the cider had loosened her up.

I never mentioned Atlantis, Arcadia, vampires or goths in front of Mrs. Howell, who did seem to taking some comfort from the fact that I didn't have dyed-black hair. Sheena seemed to be taking some care not to leave me alone with the other members of her family, but the human bladder has its limitations, and Mrs. Howell was obvious keen to snatch a private word before I managed to escape. When she did manage to corner me, she said: "I hope you'll be patient with Suzy. She's often unwell, you know, and her imagination sometimes runs away with her."

"She's been fine lately," I assured her, "and I love her imagination." It was the truth, and nothing but, if not quite the whole truth. I adored her pliant fleshy reality as well as her runaway imagination, and saw no need to separate the two in my own mind, even if diplomacy circumscribed what I could say to her mother.

We managed to escape at half past ten. Sheena made a show of having to see me home and muttered vaguely about getting a taxi back, although no one was really under the illusion that she had any intention of coming back. We could have stayed on the bus all the way into town and then got another outward-bounder practically to the door, but it was easier and a little quicker to get off opposite Rookwood Recreation Ground and walk up Harehills Lane, so that's what we decided to do.

"Well," I said, on the way, "if ever my Mum approaches you about springing a surprise birthday party for me, you have my permission to tell her to go jump off Wigan Pier."

"I wouldn't dream of it," she said. "What did Mum say to you when she got you alone?"

"Nothing much," I assured her. "Just to be sure to treat you gently."

She sighed. "Everyone always wants everyone to treat me gently," she said. "I suppose I have been ill a lot, in the past, but I'm better now. Still, at least there's no one left to add a further echo to the chorus."

That wasn't true, of course. There was one person left to do exactly that, and with musical accompaniment. I had got through one circle of purgatory unscathed, but there was another one to go, the very next day, on what I was already thinking of, privately as "bloody Sunday." Evidently, either Sheena didn't think of Davy as a member of the chorus, or she didn't think that it was his prerogative to tell me to treat her gently, given that he presumably hadn't—not gently enough, at any rate.

I'd expected another nondescript terraced house in lesser suburbia, but it turned out that Davy lived south of the railway and west of the ring road, off Whitkirk High Street. He lived in what had once been a single-storey detached cottage in the long-gone days when Whitkirk was a village. It must have been worth nearly a hundred thou. When I raised my eyebrows Sheena explained, slightly shamefacedly, that Davy rented it from his uncle.

"He's the black sheep of the family, in a way," she said, "but they haven't completely cut him off."

The incompleteness of that severance was equally obvious in the interior, not so much in the cheesy 1940s furniture that wasn't quite old enough to qualify as antique, as in the equipment that Davy had installed to assist him in pursuit of the vocation that his parents probably thought of as "Bohemian." He had a computer with at least twice the clout of mine, three heavy-duty keyboards, amps the size of sideboards and various accessories I couldn't even put a name to.

The shock of Davy's surroundings was almost matched by the man himself. I had somehow begun thinking of Davy as "wee Davy," perhaps as a subconscious strategy to minimize the vague threat his existence seemed to posed to the prospects of my future happiness, and perhaps because I had adjusted him to the same scale as Sheena. In fact he turned out to be anything but wee. I don't think of myself as unduly short, by Yorkshire standards, but he towered over me by a good five inches, and his exceedingly long black hair seemed to exaggerate the advantage.

He wasn't exactly handsome, especially with the bags under his eyes that made him look as if he hadn't slept for a week, but he was imposing. He looked more like a young Howard Stern than your average primped-up goth boy, and he moved with a stately unhurriedness that suggested that he was seriously laid back. I tried telling myself that he'd probably smoked far too much dope since deciding to cultivate his black sheep status in earnest, but I knew that it was a hopeful invention. Somehow, he reminded me of one of those spindly nocturnal proto-primates that you sometimes see in zoos: a slow loris, writ large. He was probably a year or two younger than me, although he certainly didn't look it.

"Kirk," he echoed, when Sheena introduced us, somehow giving the impression, although he didn't actually say anything, that the name awoke echoes of *Star Trek* in his mind. His voice was a profound baritone, which added a little more dignity to the name than it had ever possessed in anyone else's mouth, but also a little more absurdity. Sheena immediately retreated to the kitchen—a real kitchen, not a glorified cupboard like the one bundled into a spare corner of my flat—in order to make coffee.

"Sheena's told me a lot about you," I said, foolishly. "I liked the tapes."

"It's only half-cooked," he said, apologetically, "but it's coming along. I think I'm almost there. I hope you won't be too bored while Sheen and I get on with things."

*Sheen!* I thought. *She told me that she was Sheena to everybody. Apparently not.*

"No, that's okay," I said. "She warned me that you'd be working. I won't get in the way."

He leaned closer, exaggerating the looming effect. He seemed to be looking down at me from a mountainous height. Knowing that it was just an optical illusion didn't make it any more comfortable.

"There's no polite way to say this," he whispered, "so I'll just come right out with it. If you're pissing Sheen about, and you don't stop right away, I'll come after you and rip your fucking head off."

I'd heard of people's jaws dropping in amazement, but I'd never experienced it until then. The only reply I could contrive was a strangled: "I'm not." What I thought was that it was a bloody cheek, coming from someone who'd evidently pissed her about himself…except, of course, that I didn't know the exact circumstances of their break-up, and they still seemed to be getting along perfectly adequately music-wise. Obviously, like practically everybody else, he still felt entitled feel protective and act the part.

"Because," he added, without any evident change of mental gear, "you could be really good for her, you know, if you're serious. She needs someone serious."

"Right," I said. It never even occurred to me to try to look for some smart line with which to come back at him. Extrapolating to the surreal was definitely not called for in this instance. I knew it was a man-to-man thing, although it wasn't like any man-to-man thing I had ever encountered before. "I'm serious."

He nodded his huge-seeming head and politely retreated to the margins of what we in Yorkshire consider to be a man's personal space. Then he retreated an extra step, as if to emphasize that he needed more personal space than most.

"Everything okay?" said Sheena, as she brought in three coffee mugs, two in her right hand and one in the left.

"Peachy," I said, trying not to sound resentful. "He says he'll rip my head off if I do you wrong, but apart from that we're practically blood-brothers already."

"He'll have to join the queue, if it comes to that" Sheena said, with perfect equanimity. "Davy, behave yourself—you had your chance and dropped the ball. Don't give Kirk any hassle, or it'll be your head on the block." She turned back to me. "Don't worry—if it does come to that,

I'll get him to back off until I've had my own pound of flesh. Blood included, of course. After that, you probably wouldn't feel your head coming off. A mere *coup de grâce*."

It was no good complaining that that kind of humor was a side of her I hadn't seen before. She had a lot of sides, and I wouldn't have wanted it any other way. "Well," I said, "At least we all know where we stand, future-mutilation-wise."

"You mustn't think it's jealousy," Sheena observed, punctiliously. "Davy doesn't do jealousy. He doesn't care who I fuck. He just needs my input into the music."

"I care," said Davy, with a slight hint of injury. "I could do jealousy, too, if need be. Not the point. If you're happy, I'm happy too."

The conversation was becoming tedious, and I was glad when it lapsed. I remembered Sheena saying that I would probably like Davy, and that I'd decided to reserve my judgment. It had been a wise decision; I didn't like Davy at all. But when he started his back-up tapes running and began fingering his keyboards, I had to admit that he had a certain style. He had the amps turned up so that the music sounded far louder than it did on tape, and there was something about the acoustics of the cottage's main room that made the produce of his drum machine seem even more insistent than it ever had before. I felt it vibrating in my rib-cage, not unpleasantly by any means, but more intrusively than I could have wished.

I sat in a corner, already feeling like a specter at a feast. I knew that the feeling was only going to get worse, and that I just had to stick it out. I was certain that Sheena only had the best of motives for letting me into this part of her life, just as I was certain that Libby had only had the best of motives for hauling me into the previous one by the scruff of my neck, and I certainly wouldn't have felt good about being left out of it, but it wasn't comforting to be forced to see that Sheena already had an intimate relationship that ours—however close it might become—couldn't weaken or reduce. I was prepared to be convinced that Davy genuinely didn't envy me any part of Sheena that was actually accessible to me, but that didn't mean that I had to refrain from envying him the part of Sheena that was only accessible to him. I could do jealousy, and then some. I couldn't help myself.

I'd never seen musicians at work before, so I didn't know what to expect, but I certainly hadn't imagined that it would be so fragmentary or so repetitive. Davy would play a bit, then Sheena would supply a few words, and then they'd break off—for no particular reason that I could discern—and start again. It wouldn't have been so bad if they'd seemed to be building something that got longer and longer each time they tried it, converging on completion, but every time they seemed satisfied with the way one fragment was going they'd switch to something else. They seemed to make such switches without any significant discussion, as if by instantaneous common consent. The intensity of their communion increased by slow degrees, until they both seemed utterly lost. I wondered whether they would even notice if I got up and left, or if I started yelling at them, but I didn't want to try it in case I was right.

It would only have been horribly tedious and mildly annoying if the fragments hadn't been so loud, but I found that the assault on my ears had a peculiar progressive effect on my imagination. Even though I wasn't involved in the making of the shattered soundscape, I was sucked into it regardless. The insistent beat didn't lose its authority in being so frequently interrupted; in a curious fashion, the incompleteness of the many repetitions began to create a kind of physical need in the parts of my body that were reverberating, which gradually confused and disorientated me—but as if in answer to that penetrating loss of focus, I thought that I began to see the relationship between Sheena and Davy much more clearly.

They worked on the Byronic kiss-and-sting motif for a while, but not as long as they worked on the ramifications of "I want to be free, of myself." Davy seemed to know what it meant, or was at least prepared to pretend.

As I watched the two of them together, exploring esoteric fractions of some vaster and inchoate scheme, I began to fancy that they were both serving as Muses for one another, each drawing the other out and each changing the other's perceptions of their collaborative endeavor. I might once have thought of it as a kind of symbiosis, but I'd heard and read too much of vampires in the last couple of weeks. I couldn't help seeing it as a mutual parasitism that was taking a toll of both of them rather than working to their mutual advantage.

I tried to put such ominous thoughts aside by letting my mind wander. As the train of thought ran off, seemingly under its own steam, it got a little lighter—but it never left the realm of the macabre.

How long could a vampire survive on a desert island, I wondered, if she had only her own blood to drink?

At first, it seemed to me that her predicament wouldn't be much different from that of other hypothetical castaways, who had nothing to eat but slices carved from their own flesh and nothing to drink but their own piss, but then I remembered the difference that Sheena had taught me. To a vampire, blood isn't mere food. To a vampire, blood is life itself, and anyone who feeds a vampire is profoundly changed in the process. So the vampire castaway drinking from her own veins wouldn't simply be wasting away; she'd be embarked upon some mysterious process of self-induced metamorphosis. But suppose that on the desert island in question there was not one vampire but two, who thus had the alternative of sustaining themselves on one another's blood rather than their own. They, too, would be in a situation very different from two castaways who attempted to dine on one another's meat, or two snakes who tried to swallow one another's tails. They would be remaking one another as they fed, inducing mysterious metamorphoses of flesh and spirit alike.

If a vampire muse needed nothing but blood, I remembered saying to Sheena, during one our exploratory discussions of the subject, she surely wouldn't bother trading inspiration for what she could have for free—but if she too obtained her share of inspiration, of creativity, the trade-off would be more understandable. Not necessarily fair and equal, of course, but understandable. Even if it were a crooked game, you might have to play, if it were the only game in town.

It was all a flight of fancy, of course. Davy and Sheena were just making music, after their own conscientiously esoteric fashion. They weren't drinking one another's blood. And yet, those bags under Davy's eyes made it look as if he hadn't slept for a week, and Sheena was so slim that anyone who hadn't seen her eat a well-done steak could easily have wondered whether she might be anorexic. Now that I'd seen the bruises, I knew what a delicate flower she could be—but only *could be*, because I had her assurance that there were also times when she hardly bruised at all.

I could do jealousy, and then some. If anyone were feeding on the substance of Sheena's soul, metaphorically or supernaturally, I wanted it to be me. Obviously, I thought, Davy felt the same way, albeit coming from a slightly different direction. Allegedly, he didn't mind me fucking her, or had been instructed not to mind, but if I upset the equilibrium on which her singing depended by disappointing her, he was apparently prepared to rip my head off—always provided that he could get to the front of the queue in time.

Eventually, they finished. They seemed happy with what they'd done, although it didn't seem to me that they'd completed anything. Unfortunately, I wasn't like Big Bad Davy. It wasn't enough for me to be happy that she should be happy. For me to be happy, I had to be the *cause* of her happiness—and if that made me a kind of vampire that neither of us could admire, I had to live with it.

I knew that I couldn't woo her away from the music, and I knew that I shouldn't even try, but that didn't mean that I couldn't try to compete, to make my own demands on the blood that coursed through her body. I didn't have to settle for being the only one who was changed. I could change her too, if I only put my mind and heart into the attempt. As she'd said herself, anyone can be a vampire, and everything that we take too readily for granted is really supernatural.

Sheena went to the loo before we left and I took the opportunity to have another wee word with Big Davy.

"So who were you in a previous life?" I asked. "Beethoven or Jack the Ripper—or both?"

He grinned. "What you see is what you get," he said. "I don't do past lives, or blood rites. Do you?"

That was what I wanted to hear. I'd suspected as much. Sheena had told me that goths had a license to be weird in any way they wanted— nothing ruled out, and nothing compulsory. It not longer mattered, now whether Davy had dumped her, or she had dumped him, or whether it had been a genuinely mutual decision, when mere fucking hadn't been enough. The point was that he hadn't been able to play the game. He had, as she put it, dropped the ball, instead of even making an attempt to run with it all the way to the end-zone.

"Yes I do," I said. "And how."

He looked at me as if he didn't believe me, and as if he didn't, deep down, want to believe me, in spite of what he'd told Sheena about only wanting her to be happy. *Hypocritical cunt*, I thought.

"Well, he said, "good luck with that." He wasn't one of those people who can fake sincerity, and I'm not sure that he was even trying.

"I don't need luck," I told him. "I have imagination."

And I was sincere, although I didn't try particularly hard to put on the appearance.

After that, there was only one more purgatorial hurdle to cross, and we took it I in our stride the following weekend. By that time, I had dyed my hair, but we didn't go over the top with the rest of the apparatus. Mum just looked at me when she saw me, and sighed. Lily, bless her, was on her absolute best behavior, and didn't make a single snide remark at me, or at Sheena, even though she was wearing a low-cut off-the-shoulder dress suggestive of a desire to compete with the invader, which must have drawn some disapproving comments from Mum. I caught her studying Sheena covertly from the corner of her eyes, trying to appraise her in the light of the conflicting sets of information she had at her disposal, but she didn't seem to be doing so with any conspicuous prejudice.

Unlike Sheena, I didn't make any attempt to block any of Mum's attempts to have a word with her in private, and even facilitated it, by insisting that Lily and I would do the washing up while Mum relaxed and Sheena kept her company.

"Well," I said to Lily, when I was sure that we wouldn't be overheard, "what do you think?"

"About the hair or your girlfriend?"

"Sheena."

She shrugged her bare shoulders. "Seems okay," she said.

"High praise," I observed. "No more detail than that?"

"She seems perfectly sane," she concluded, as if reluctantly, "except, obviously, for the fact that she's smitten with you. You can see that in the way she looks at you. Or maybe that's just terrible taste in men."

"It's a good job you're joking," I said. "I bear grudges, you know."

"So do I," she said. "Must run in the family. Anyway, as long as you're happy, it's fine by me." She sounded a lot more convincing than Davy had, but it was easy for her, there being no potential jealousy issues involved.

"Thanks," I said.

"Why? You don't need my approval,"

"No, but it's nice to have it, however grudging."

"Oh, don't mind me. Since Dad died I've had to transfer my Electra complex to my brothers, and since Steve went away and you came back...." Evidently her A level syllabus didn't stick entirely to the safer parts of Freud.

"Sheena's not the only one with terrible taste in men, then?" I suggested.

She grinned wryly. "I didn't mean that, as you well know. She has great taste. Very discerning. As I said, I've seen the way she looks at you. As long as that look's in her eye, you're safe."

I wondered whether being "safe" was her top priority in considering relationships for herself, as well as for others.

"I'll trust your judgment on that one," I told her.

I didn't get such an extensive opportunity to talk to Mum on her own, but I managed to find a space of time long enough to get a synopsis of her impression.

"She's that thin," was Mum's summary verdict, spoken while shaking her head sadly "but it seems to be the fashion nowadays. Look at that Ally McBeal." The last remark was not a veiled reference to Sheena's talent for invention, but merely evidence of the censorious frame of mind in which Mum invariably watched TV.

When we left to go back to Harehills, I asked Sheena whether Mum had given her the third degree.

"No," she said. "We chatted about the most banal subjects in the world. No warnings, and no probing. She does seem to regret that you don't have an ironing board, but she didn't go so far as to suggest that I might like to get one if I'll be doing all your ironing in the future—which I won't, by the way."

"That's Mum," I said. "A paragon of tact and diplomacy, albeit with an unhealthy fixation on cleaning products. What did you think of Lily?"

"She's sweet, although she kept looking at me suspiciously, as if I might be hiding some terrible secret. Does she dress like that all the time?"

"Certainly not. I didn't even know she had an outfit like that. I'm surprised Mum didn't make her change before we arrived."

"Did I pass the inspection, do you think?"

"Of course," I said. "Now that she's met you, all possible misconceptions are out of the way. She'll love you like a sister."

"A little less oppressively than my actual sister, I hope. It might be nice to have someone around to whom I can feel protective, for a change."

"Lily doesn't need protecting."

"Neither do I, but it doesn't stop people. Does it stop you—with regard to Lily, I mean?"

"I suppose it doesn't stop the feeling—or the feeling of helplessness because I know that there's nothing I can actually do to provide her with useful protection. I imagine Libby feels the same way. So, what are we going to do with what's left of the evening?"

"Back to the flat," she said. "Atlantis first, then bed."

I took due note of the fact that she'd said *the* flat and not *your* flat. She hadn't actually moved in, as yet—not formally, at any rate—but she was already thinking of it as a home from home, or simply as a home.

# XII

All the predictions about work proved justified. For three days our relationship was the only topic of conversation, and the target of all giggles and gibes. Then it just faded into the background and become part of the everyday landscape, hardly worthy of attention. The black-dyed hair generated a few supposedly-witty comments, but no surprise at all.

In the next few weeks Sheena and I went dog racing at Elland Road and horseracing at Wetherby. We went dancing in places where there were dark-clad bands playing to legions of dark-clad acolytes, and Sheena introduced me to the drinking dens where the goth crowd hung out. She made sure that I fitted in, appearance wise, and everyone there seemed very easy-going; it was certainly less fractious than a girls' night out in the Black Boar, and there was a much better class of background music.

Mostly, however, we stayed in and "went to Atlantis"—which, for the purposes of the shorthand phrase, included Arcadia and occasional other locations—and gradually, the intervals between the mundane excursions grew longer.

There were no blood-rites, as yet; I came to the conclusion after a week or two that vampirism was something to which I would probably have to graduate, once I had done the appropriate course-work and passed the requisite exams.

While I was still figuring out the best way to work it, for her benefit rather than mine, I let Sheena do most of the talking. The kind of self-hypnosis she practiced wasn't much more complicated than relaxing into a mental gear somewhere west of neutral, and once I'd learned how not to be an inhibitory presence she didn't have any obvious difficulty in getting there, or in free-associating fantasies of quite extraordinary elaboration.

Copying her was no problem either. She knew that I was faking it at first, but she told me that it was perfectly all right, because the more intently and cleverly I faked it, the closer I would get to slipping over the edge, so that the fake would mutate insensibly into the real, and I would actually start dreaming past lives, and making fruitful contact with other fragments of the universal soul.

"Just let your imagination go," she said. "Just let it run free. At first, your conscious mind will invent things, but the things you invent will develop a momentum of their own, and will gradually free themselves from your direction. Little by little, your unconscious mind will take over, feeding you the imagery spontaneously, and when you're completely immersed, when the unconscious is doing its own thing, material will begin to creep in from more distant locations.

I discovered soon enough that Sheena was right about the nature of the creative process—that it really did seem that I was finding the material I fed in, not in the books that I read by way of research and helpful prompting, but within the fantasy itself, as if they had always been there waiting to be noticed or uncovered. It was perhaps as well, because the Atlantis she wove out of the provisions of her fertile unconscious wasn't much like any of the Atlantises in the books I was able to borrow or buy—which ranged from Plato to Madame Blavatsky—and the Arcadia would have been hardly recognizable to the scrupulous author of *Dr. Smith's Classical Dictionary*.

It was inevitable, of course, that the fantasies I was improvising while in search of authentic remembrance would come to occupy much of my thought even when I was not with Sheena. At work, where I was now able to cruise through calls on autopilot, having engaged my telephone personality, I often found myself slipping away into daydreams of discovery, in which I would conjure up new tidbits of information and imagery that fit one or other of the jigsaws we were patiently bringing towards completion. Whenever Sheena was working with Davy, or visiting her mother and sister, or out shopping, or doing whatever mysterious things it is that compel lasses to spend ten times as long in the bathroom as lads, Atlantis and Arcadia were always there to provide me with temporary avenues of escape. Bit by bit, slyly and shyly, they even managed to invade my dreams, and even sleep became part of the heroic quest, the search for the grail.

The sex was even better once we began to take it for granted, although I did try to be as gentle as possible, even when Sheena told me that she was in one of her non-bruising phases. For me—but not, I suspect, for her—the sex functioned in the beginning as a kind of anchor in reality, tethering the flights of fancy that became, in essence, a leisurely kind of foreplay. I thought of the sex, to begin with, as "coming down to earth" after an excursion into what I sometimes referred to mentally as Neverland, and it wasn't difficult to draw that distinction while our mutual hypnosis sessions weren't authentically mutual at all. While we were exploring past lives sitting at a table, or in two chairs placed so that we could stare into one another's eyes, the act of going to bed was always an obvious transition from one state of mind to another.

That artifice only lasted for a couple of weeks or so, though—time for me to adapt psychologically to the conventionality of what we were doing. As time went by, we began to indulge our flights of fancy while lying together on the couch. Sometimes we went to bed before we began to explore the still-hidden treasures of Sheena's supposed memories, and added the physical into the imaginary as if one could be subtly dissolved into the other without any the crossing of any obvious boundary. I had no alternative, then, but to enter more fully into the fantasies myself—but why would I have wanted an alternative? An alternative was the very opposite of what I wanted.

It was natural enough, during my early attempts to help Sheena recall her supposed past lives in Atlantis and Arcadia, for me to ask her whether there was anyone already among her past selves' acquaintances that might be one of my own former incarnations, and which I could simply "move in to," rather than trying to make contact with someone unfamiliar to her. She denied it with such apparent assurance that I never thought the point worth pressing. I did wonder, briefly, if her confident denials were a way of keeping me distant from the deep core of her dream, but that wasn't the case, and I soon became convinced of it. She was just as emphatic that none of Davy's previous incarnations was present, even though Atlantis and Arcadia were both places where music flourished. In Sheena's Atlantis, in fact, choral singing was the highest art, much more vital to the coherence and solidarity of society than religion.

"I wish I could sing the songs of Atlantis for you," she said, "but I can't. I've tried before"—I presumed she meant that she had tried to sing them for Davy—"and it can't be done. The language of Atlantis is dead, and I can't pronounce the words, but even if I could, they're not the kind of songs that can be sung solo."

That was, of course, one of the many aspects of her fantasies that were intrinsically mysterious. For instance, her memories of Atlantis were all night-time memories, although her memories of being a dryad or an Amazon in Arcadia were usually sunlit, pleasantly if not gloriously. According to Sheena, that wasn't because Sharayah or Morgina—the two Atlanteans she remembered most frequently and most clearly—were the kind of vampires who might be shriveled by exposure to the sun, although they were both been vampires in the strange and slight elusive fashion with which Sheena had replaced the Stokerian mythology, but because they were deliberately shielding their memories of day from her miraculous hindsight.

"Our past selves can do that," she explained. "Access to such memories is a privilege, not a right. In fact, access to our own memories is a privilege too. Sometimes, when we repress aspects of our present histories, it's not because they're traumatic in themselves but because they're linked to recurrent patterns extending across the centuries, like wormholes."

"But why would they deliberately shield their memories of daylight hours, if they really can expose themselves to the sun?" I asked.

"I'm not sure, exactly," she confessed. "Perhaps they think they're protecting me. Perhaps they really are—unlike my sister."

"There might be something terrible in Atlantis that can only be seen by day," I suggested, valiantly doing my best to help feed her greedy imagination. "Some monster that retires to its lair at sunset and returns at dawn, like a movie vampire in reverse, which they might consider to terrible for the likes of us to behold."

"It can't be anything as crude as that," she assured me, tacitly criticizing the quality of my masculine imagination. "I think it might be something to do with color. At night, no matter how bright the stars are, it's very difficult to perceive color. Candlelight helps, but it's not like real daylight. I think the Atlanteans may have had more colors than we have, and that Sharayah and Morgina don't want me to realize what we've lost."

"Perhaps that's why the magical creatures of Arcadia were destined to die out," I suggested, still trying to help. "We might flatter ourselves that satyrs and centaurs, dryads and the gods themselves faded out of existence when humans ceased to believe in them, but it's hard to see why they'd be impressed by our skepticism. Perhaps their hearts were broken, although they didn't know why, by the loss of the secret colors of Atlantis. Perhaps that's why they lost the ability to sing in proper harmony, or even to speak in the language of the authentic Golden Age. Did the Arcadians invent art and drama in the hope of being able to rebuild what they dimly remembered? And is that why the arts have been going downhill ever since, as the memory is slowly obscured from all but a frustrated few? Except, of course, that you're not frustrated, are you?"

"No," she said, apparently ignoring the *double entendre*—but perhaps not. "What I do remember only brings me a little closer to completion."

There's nothing in the least surprising in the fact that I really did began to hypnotize myself with the same fancies, occasionally slipping into a mental gear where disbelief was totally suspended. The only real cause for surprise is that I couldn't make any progress inventing or summoning up the memories of any past lives of my own. I wanted to find my Atlantean and Arcadian selves, even if it turned out that they didn't overlap in time with any of Sheena's selves and couldn't actually meet, but it seemed that I was to be limited to the role of disembodied voice, accompanying Sheena when she flew upon the wings of time, a mere parasite of her remembrance.

"I wish I could be more," I told her, more than once.

"Don't worry about it," she advised. "What was, was—the past is unchangeable. It's not the worst of fates, to be a passenger in my memories for a little while. It's a far easier way to my heart. I do wish you could hear, though, if only for a moment, the song of Atlantis, the song of the world as it was. I can describe the people to you, the buildings, the flowers and the animals. I can even describe the chimeras and the spirits, at least as they seem by moonlight, but I can't describe the music, because that can't be put into any words we know."

"I have more than enough," I assured her, repenting of the suggestion that I could be in any way dissatisfied with our relationship. "I have everything I need."

I had, too. I had everything I needed.

Fortunately, my own imagination seemed to prove equal to the continual challenge of improvising ideas that were coherent with Sheena's images of Atlantis and Arcadia. I soon got past fatuous speculations of the kind in which I'd indulged at Davy's house, concerning vampires on desert islands, because the vampires of Atlantis, as Sheena imagined it, weren't like that at all. In any case, it was easier, to begin with, not to grapple with the supernatural aspects of her fantasy at all, but to focus more narrowly on the material ones, and to address the predicament of Sheena's "prime template"—the self that was, in some sense, the archetype of all the other affiliate selves distributed through the historical and mythical landscape.

Shena's prime template was the Atlantean named Morgina, even though she had lived in a later period of the history of the lost continent than Sharayah—prime status was apparently not dependent on strict chronological order. Morgina was a high priestess and a great scholar. She was living in a period when the numerous volcanoes of Atlantis had been quiescent for a long period, although by to means extinct, and when earthquakes were relatively rare and way down on whatever equivalent of the Richter scale the Atlanteans had.

One of the consequences of the long period of stability had been an increase in agricultural production and population, and a relative shift of power from the priestly elite, who had once held a virtual monopoly on literacy and learning, to secular powers, associated with the growth of various schismatic cults. After a particularly violent dynastic dispute, in which the rebels seeking to overturn the old regime had embraced an unorthodox set of beliefs for reasons of political expediency, Morgina had been arrested and imprisoned—not in a dungeon, and certainly not in chains, but something more akin to house arrest. She was allowed to keep her books and to continue with her scholarly investigations and experiments in magic, but always under close surveillance, and always in danger of having her privileges evoked or—far worse—being quietly scheduled for sly assassination.

Atlantean priestesses were not permitted to marry, in order that the cult to which they belonged retained a monopoly on their movable and immovable property, but they were not required to remain virginal, and most had lovers, usually politicians or military leaders who provided them with the alliance of secular muscle in exchange for the backing of religious authority. Morgina's lover had, however, been murdered during the power-seizure that had led to her imprisonment, and her relationships with contemporary males were carefully restricted, not merely for the purpose of denying her the alliance of armed might, but also in order to starve her of the spiritual nourishment of blood. Any man who even seemed to be getting to close to her would have been in danger of assassination.

Because inheritance in Atlantis was matrilineal, there being no official legal recognition of paternity, although the society was far from matriarchal, the sisters of monarchs and other powerful individuals tended to be very influential, and often became priestesses and/or magiciennes themselves—the two were usually, but not necessarily, the same thing. Havren, the usurper king who was keeping Morgina imprisoned, had no female lover, but he did have a sister who was, in large measure, the power behind the throne, albeit one required to move in relatively mysterious and magical ways. Her name was Osselina, and she was, in crude terms, Morgina's arch-enemy, although she always pretended a perverse friendship, because she was avid to win possession of Morgina's magical secrets. For that purpose she had tried to arrange a political relationship between her brother and Morgina, but Havren was unenthusiastic about the idea and Morgina hated it, so Osselina's tactics had gradually switched from politics to pressure, both physical and magical.

That was the somewhat painful situation in which Sheena found herself when she made contact with Morgina in her hypnotic state, but she nevertheless favored that contact more than any other. Identifying with Amazons, dryads and Sharayah seemed to me to be much more inherently attractive, or at least much less paranoid, but Morgina was her principal alter ego, her prime template, in some strange sense more her than she was herself, and uniquely precious for that reason.

It was, of course, all in her mind, and could easily have been reckoned a fantasy, crying out for psychoanalytical interpretation, but even if I had wanted to approach it in that fashion, which I didn't, what psychoanalytic scheme should I have employed? Freudian? Jungian? Eric Berne's game theory? Abraham Maslow's theory of self-actualization? They were all just fantasies for the pseudoexplanation of other fantasies, perhaps not vicious circles, but ones that didn't lead anywhere. The fantasies themselves, by contrast, did lead somewhere, both for Sheena, who was creating them, and for me, who was following them. They led us both where we wanted to go, and the fact that we were going together increased their value a hundredfold, for both of us.

Isn't that, when you cut through all the bullshit, what love really is?

Sheena didn't mind that possibility that it was all a fantasy being put to her. "Of course it's a fantasy, Kirk," she said. "The entire material universe is just a fantasy of the universal soul; matter is just an aspect of its dreaming. In getting in touch with the universal soul via the depths of the unconscious, we're entering into the scheme of that fantasy."

Which is, in essence, probably what I just said, in different terminology.

Fundamentally, it was a matter of love: the ultimate fantasy of the universal soul, the most precious illusion of all.

"If you can enter the history of Atlantis at various points," I said, by way of extrapolating her notions, "surely you could find out what eventually happened to Morgina by consulting a viewpoint further along the timeline. Sharayah is earlier, but wouldn't it be possible to find another past self more recent?"

"Perhaps," she said, "but I haven't done it yet."

"On the other hand," I suggested, "why can't you make contact with Morgina's intellect at any point in her life, including the end. Why do you seem to be tracking her experiences in chronological order, instead of making contact with it at different points during her life, without regard to its sequence?"

"It doesn't work like that," she told me—a statement that recurred in our relationship with the occasionally-irritating repetitiveness of a chirping cricket or a dripping tap. "Every time I make new contact with Morgina, and become Morgina, it has to be a Morgina further along in her life than the last time. It's not the case that the number of days that have elapsed in my life equal the number of days that have elapsed in hers—sometimes only a few minutes have elapsed in her experience, and sometimes much longer, but I can't affiliate with her consciousness in an earlier phase than when I last melded with it. As for knowing what happened to her from the subsequent historical record, I already know that she died, because everyone does, and if I knew what history recorded about the manner of her death, I wouldn't necessarily be any closer to the truth, because historians often lie for political reasons, and even if they record the circumstances correctly, that doesn't necessarily offer any indication as to what happened to her soul after death. She was a powerful magicienne, after all, and an accomplished vampire. That's why she has affinities with so many future affiliates. In a sense, my existence could be considered a fragment of her afterlife."

I was beginning, by then, to get a sense of the overall pattern. "But in addition to other material affiliates—her future lives, or your past lives—she…and, logically, you…also has echoes that take the form, if one can use the term form, of a vampiric *spirit*: something immaterial that can nevertheless interact with matter, drawing life-force from the blood of both affiliated and non-affiliated individuals?"

"That's right," she replied, pleased with my progress.

"And Morgina's magical research is devoted to securing and furnishing that kind of posthumous future or self?"

"Among other things. If she were only concerned with herself, perhaps most, if not all of her endeavor would be devoted to that end, but she also has political concerns—an interest in the future of her cult, its secular connections, and Atlantis itself. In consequence, much of her research, at least clandestinely, is devoted to trying to hinder the persecutions of Havren and Osselina, further the schemes of her former allies, and stimulate new forces of opposition, internal and external."

"She doesn't know, then, that in the fullness of time, it's all futile, because Atlantis is going to sink in its entirety?"

"Yes, she does know that, although she doesn't know exactly when it will happen. Everyone is Atlantis who trusts the adepts knows that the sinking is ultimately inevitable, and various parties are trying to prepare for that in different ways, either by fostering the technological progress that will hopefully allow the development of powered flight, by hastening the colonization of the continents, by opening up escape routes for posthumous entities, or developing spells or technologies capable of delaying the catastrophe."

"Why powered flight?" I asked. "What's wrong with ships?"

"Nothing," she said. "It's by means of ships that they're establishing colonies on the continental coasts, although it's a difficult task. But when the catastrophe finally comes, the associated tidal waves will—did, that is—make navigation extremely difficult, if not impossible, and the vast majority of the ships went down with everything else. The associated atmospheric disturbances made aerial escape difficult too, and history has no record, so we don't know, and my affiliates through the ages have never known, whether any Atlanteans escaped by that route, or where they ended up if they did."

"And by the same token," I supplied, "the tidal waves caused by the quakes and eruptions devastated a great many of the colonies on the African and American coasts."

"Exactly," said Sheena. "Volcanic eruptions and quakes in the Mediterranean, and their associated marine and atmospheric phenomena, devastated Arcadia in the same way. The Minoan civilization suffered a similar catastrophe, on a smaller scale."

"And because oral tradition invariably contacts and collapses distant memories, compressing the actual timescale and complexity of events, such fugitive accounts of these various catastrophes as were handed down were gradually eroded, and ultimately fused, so that instead of recalling a series of Deluge-type events spread over hundreds of thousands of years, the earliest written records condensed the entire inheritance into one single Deluge recalled and represented in a cartoonish fashion?"

"The earliest written records still extant," she said. "Many previous ones had perished long before, completely wiped out. You're beginning to get the picture, though. The Muse is beginning to get to work, as you can see. You get a little flash of enlightenment when you come up with ideas like that, don't you?

I got a little flash of something, but I suspected that it was simply pride in my own ability to tart things up—pride greatly enhanced by her approval. But what did it matter, at the end of the day? So long as she was happy, I was happy—and not just because the sex was still great: because I really did think that we were making progress in the relationship, and in our love. Maybe it was just a *folie à deux*, but what is any love affair, in essence, but a kind of *folie à deux*. Tristan and Isolde? Antony and Cleopatra? Burton and Taylor? If it was madness, who could possibly have wished to be sane?

We were happy—and how many sane people could say that? Trudi? Jez? Davy? Lily? Mum? I didn't think so. So far as I could see and feel, in fact, we were practically the only happy people in the world, or at the very least the happiest of the happy. And what made it even better was that there was further progress still to be made, further ecstasy still to be claimed. Thus far, as I was only a learner, not yet fully initiated, not yet a vampire, not yet bound by blood to Sheena, her affiliates and my own, linked to the universal soul by the ultimate communion.

I tried, of course, to invent or discover other selves for myself, not only in Arcadia and Atlantis, but in the shadowy recesses of what passes for history, but is, of course, mostly lies and other people's inventions. The latter seemed easier, because I had raw material with which to work.

I tried briefly to reinvent myself in my imagination as Silius, Messalina's lover, whose alleged bigamous marriage to her had brought about her execution, but I soon gave up on that one, partly because I couldn't quite cast myself with any conviction as a Roman senator, and partly because it seemed, somehow, as if I were not only trying to be unfaithful to Sheena but trying to be unfaithful to her with one of Trudi's affiliates, which would have been adding insult to injury. I tried Mark Antony too, but felt that I was just being silly. I tried being a druid bard, but I was too acutely conscious of the fact that I didn't know a single word of Welsh or Breton, and the known reality of those arcane languages interfered with the imaginative endeavor.

I decided, in the end—as I suspected that Sheena had also decided, consciously or unconsciously, at an early phase in the evolution of her own supernatural consciousness, to push the kind of history that had already been fantasized by other people, under the slight pressure of lived reality, into the background, and concentrate the bulk of my own imaginative effort on the regions of "history" about which virtually nothing was known. I attempted to be a herdsman in Arcadia, but that was essentially tedious, and casting myself as a satyr was simply too much of a stretch, not so much for my physical modesty as my intellectual arrogance.

When I explained those difficulties to Sheena, of course—because I wanted to be entirely honest with her—she told me that they were entirely expectable hitches on the path to true remembrance, the gradual metamorphosis of conscious fakery into unconscious authenticity.

By degrees, therefore, I began to focus more exclusively on the process of using Sheena's remembrances as the raw material for my own. In particular, I tried to invent lovers for her affiliates in Arcadia and Atlantis, in order simultaneously to maintain plausibility and fidelity. Most of all, I tried to invent a lover for Morgina, who was conspicuously devoid of one, who desperately needed one to feed her longing for blood, and who still had room for one in the fiction of her life posterior to Sheena's running associations, provided that I could invent a story by means of which he could dodge the restrictions and surveillance placed upon her by Havren and Osselina.

Sheena approved wholeheartedly of that attempt, but she didn't seem to go out of her way to make it easy for me—quite the reverse, in fact. When I came up with new subplots that might enable a lover to make contact with Morgina, Sheena generally managed to find some flaw in the plan—and when she didn't have a flaw already built into the complex notion of how Morgina's situation was organized, it seemed to me that she introduced a new complication.

By then, we'd persuaded the staff of the HR department at the center to rig the shift-schedule so that we were almost always on identical shifts. In our company, unlike those where workplace relationships are proscribed or frowned upon, Human Resources tried to live up to their name, and were not unsympathetic to the appeals of true love. That facilitated our explorations of the past and one another. Even so, it took me several attempts, spread over a similar number of days, to figure out that something odd was going on with regard to my attempts to set up some kind of a transtemporal link with Morgina.

From Sheena's point of view, I figured, it was a crucial hurdle that I had to get over in order to make the transition from fakery to authenticity, and even if that supposed difference was really all in her mind, and purely symbolic, it was vital. It was a challenge that I had to meet, and perhaps the ultimate one.

One way or another, I thought, I needed to invent or discover a hero capable of getting through to Sheena's "prime template." In continually raising obstacles to my inventions she wasn't trying to stop me doing that, she was just trying to make sure that I did it *right*, and she was surely entitled to do that, because that, after all, is the very essence of romance: the hero has to win the heroine, fair and square; the holy grail has to be earned; you can't just fuck your way to it, the way some people seem to think.

I invented clever spies, noble knights, ingenious tricksters, accomplished bards and superheroic blond Vikings cast away on the Atlantean shore after heroic journeys from proto-Scandinavia, but none of them worked. The Viking very nearly made it, but Osselina managed to invent a love potion that made him fall in love with her, and Morgina's magic, powerful as it was, was insufficient to break the spell.

Frustration was beginning to set in, and I cursed myself or my slowness, because I obviously wasn't good enough at self-hypnosis, and I just couldn't break through from making things up consciously to finding them ready-made in the utmost depths of the unconscious—or, at least, not finding the *right* things buried deep in my unconscious. Sheena didn't get impatient, though, and she didn't hold my incompetence against me. She was all kindness, all consolation, and even tried to take some of the blame on to herself.

"If I were a better teacher," she said, "you'd be making faster progress. There's certainly no fault in your motivation. I know that you love me; I can't doubt that any longer."

"It's not you," I insisted, "it's me. I do love you, with all my heart, but I can't quite seem to come up with the answer to the conundrum. It's not the balls I lack, but something else—something to cut through the bullshit and get down to the quick."

"I think you're right," she said. "We need to cut through the problem. We shouldn't put it off any longer. It's time for the blood rite. It's time for you to become a vampire. Are you ready for that?"

I had grown accustomed to assuming that I'd have to get over the barrier that was keeping me from making proper contact with my past lives before we proceeded to that, but I realized that there was no logical reason why either accomplishment had to precede the other—and the exchange of blood might easily be exactly the stimulus I needed to complete the other aspect of the communion.

"Yes I am," I said. "When?"

"Tomorrow night," she said.

"It's a date."

And just like that, it was settled: the alchemical wedding; the fusion of souls; the rite that would make us one in the womb of the universal soul and bind us together forever.

# XIII

I cooked dinner—steak, just as on the first occasion, because it's good to have traditions, to build patterns in time, to increase the coherency of life within the tiny margin of control that we have—and we drank a nice bottle of red wine, which didn't last, this time, until we had finished the cheesecake, so we had a glass of brandy as well. With two of us sharing the household expenses, we could stretch to luxuries like that. Afterwards, we cuddled for a while on the couch while listening to the Fields of the Nephilim's *Elizium* and Ataraxia's *Lost Atlantis*—just leisurely foreplay, nothing heavy. Then we went into the bedroom, where the razor blades were already set out on the bedside table.

We were careful. Sheena had a little spirit lamp, and she sterilized the first blade very carefully by holding it in the heart of the flame. While she did that, she said:

"You do know what this means, don't you, Kirk?"

"Yes," I said—but she wanted to be sure.

"This is commitment," she said. You can stop at any time, even after I've licked your blood, but if you go through to the end—once you've licked mine—we'll be united by a sacred bond, that won't just last until the end of this life, but forever. You're not a vampire yet, but once you are, there's no going back. Once we've made the exchange, the union is unbreakable."

"I know," I said.

"So, for the last time, are you perfectly certain that you want this?"

I looked at her: at her hair, he eyes, her mouth, her throat, her naked breasts, her scars, her heart...the whole ensemble. She was more than beautiful, more even than the tender matter displayed to my loving eyes. She was the universal soul made manifest, made flesh.

"Perfectly."

And she cut me, with the sterile blade, below my left nipple, where she thought the heart ought to be beating, on the other side of the rib cage.

For the first couple of seconds, I didn't feel the cut. Then the blood began to ooze out, in a thin, exceedingly delicate line, about an inch long. Then I felt the sting, but it was very slight—and when she bent over, and put her lips to the cut, and I felt her tongue slide along the cut, the pain was transformed, and was no longer pain at all. It didn't become pleasure—nothing as simple as that. It became a kind of feeling I'd never experienced before.

It was in my imagination, of course, because that's where all feeling is, but that didn't mean that it wasn't real. Quite the contrary; I felt in fact, that it was not only the most real sensation I'd ever experienced, but the only one. All the others, I thought, had been mere twinges of the neurons, just mental echoes of the physical. That one was real. That donation of blood, that donation to Sheena, to my vampire Muse, went beyond the physical, through the utmost depths of the collective unconscious, and opened up a world to me.

When she raised her head again, she reached for a piece of cotton wool that she'd carefully placed on the beside table and dipped a corner into a sugar-bowl containing an inch of water that she'd poured from a bottle that had been in the fridge. She applied the cold compress to the cut, and held it there. The seconds stretched to more than a minute. The cotton wool took on a slight red stain, but when she took it away, the bleeding had stopped.

"Your turn," she said.

Did I hesitate? Did she only expect me to hesitate? At any rate, she added: "I can do it, if don't want to make the cut—as long as you lick the blood."

"It's all right," I told her. "I can make the cut."

"Good," she said. She wanted me to make the cut. She'd only every cut herself before, I knew. She wasn't a virgin in the conventional sense, but she'd never shared her blood—how could she, when she knew full well that it would seal an unbreakable bond? She knew that it was something she could only ever do once, and this was the once.

She loved me. She wanted us to be together, forever.

I sterilized the second blade. It was just a ritual, I knew. The human mouth is full of bacteria. The blade might be sterile, but my lips and tongue weren't, and couldn't be—but the ritual was what mattered; the symbolic gesture was what mattered.

I looked very carefully at the skin where the underside of her breast curved away, searching for an area of flesh where an inch-long scar could be drawn without intersecting with any of the faint scars that were there already. She was lying back on the bed, with her eyes closed, but she opened them briefly to look into mine, and make sure of me.

"Do it," she said.

I drew the line, taking immense care to make the slightest possible cut, with hardly any depth at all—just deep enough to draw blood, and not a nanometer deeper—at least, I had that precision in my imagination. Then I lowered my head, and put my mouth to the wound.

I didn't expect to feel anything except for taste sensations, and I expected those to be slightly metallic, and perhaps slightly salty, or maybe sweet, but I must have been so hyped up on adrenaline that my mind was kinesthetically confused. I felt a thrill like an electric shock. My mouth seemed to fill with blood, and then my entire being seemed to fill with blood.

I had nothing in my veins but Sheena, nothing in my heart; all the movement within me, all the movement that was my life, was Sheena.

Then I dipped the cotton wool in the cold water, and applied it to the wound. Her eyes were still closed.

The cotton wool turned bright red, and was doubly soaked. I dropped it beside the bed, and seized anther piece, dipped it…and panicked. The bleeding showed no sign of stopping.

She couldn't see my panic, but she must have felt it, because she grabbed my head in both hands and held it.

"It's okay," she said. "It sometimes does that. I'm glad it did. I was afraid I might not bleed at all. I wanted you to have the blood. I needed you to have the blood. Don't worry. It'll stop. It always does. Sometimes, it just take a little longer.

My hand was shaking, but I kept applying the cotton wool.

She was right. Eventually, the blood clotted and the bleeding stopped—but it seemed to need an awful lot of cotton wool.

"I didn't mean to hurt you," I said, weakly.

"You didn't hurt me," she told me. "You know that it doesn't hurt. You know what it's really like—because we're the same now. We're fragments of the universal soul, fused together. We have an understanding…don't we?"

We did. We had an understanding.

We had sex, too, but she had to go on top, because I was too afraid of hurting her, too afraid of crushing her, too afraid of opening her wound, if I weighed upon her. She preferred it that way anyway, because it was easier for her to come. Then we went to sleep in one another's arms.

In the morning, we went to work, put on our telephone personalities, and abnormal life resumed, following its stereotype course. Nothing had changed, in the center or in the world. Only we had changed.

But not completely.

I had been expecting a breakthrough. Because everything had changed, manifestly and truly, I thought it would become easy to remember, that the clouds would have rolled away, and that I would simply *know*, because my subconscious would tell me, how my vampire self could manifest itself in Atlantis and save Morgina.

It didn't happen. I didn't remember anyone. I couldn't even make something up. On that particular issue, my imagination seemed to have run dry, as if a cold compress had been applied to it and its flow had stopped, obediently.

"It doesn't matter," Sheena assured me. "We have all the time in the world. Time isn't what it seems—you know that. It will come. You're too wound up at present; you can't relax. It's my fault, for pushing you too hard. But now we're united, now we've shared our blood, now your blood is mine and mine is yours, it's bound to happen. The connection is made; it just has to work itself out. Just relax, let yourself drift. I'm not going anywhere.

"I'll always be here, even when I'm working on the music, even when I'm at the center, taking an infinite series of irate customers through their petty problems. Spiritually, I'm with you forever now, in everyday time and eternity, in your flesh and in your dreams. You don't have to remember everything at once, in your time-anchored consciousness. In eternity, you've already remembered, and always have remembered. In eternity, everything has already happened, and everything is still to happen.

"We have our bearings now; it's just a matter of waiting for our particular journey to end. The archetypal union has already taken place, and always had; we were always an echo of it. We've completed our part of the ritual. All we have to do is be patient. It would be a dull world if everything happened at once, and left us entirely without suspense."

I knew she was right. She was, after all, Minerva, the goddess of wisdom, and I was her vigilant owl, her watchful symbol, waiting impatiently for the twilight in order to take wing. Our relationship was determined; we were one. It was just a matter of waiting for the last remaining piece of our personal jigsaw to fall into place.

At the risk of boring repetition, I suppose I ought to interrupt myself to ask my present self again whether, if I'd known exactly where and how that last piece was going to fall, I might have regretted having come so far, having done so much, having made such a commitment?

Absolutely not. I had the holy grail and the holy blood within my grasp. I wouldn't have traded that for the moon and the stars. Nobody would, unless they were insane.

A week later, when we'd been on a late shift and didn't get back to the flat until nearly midnight, we still wanted to go to Atlantis, just briefly, before we went to bed. We knew that we could have a lie-in the next morning. Sheena slipped into her altered state of consciousness easily enough, while I did my best to relax, but without ever losing my mundane consciousness of what was happening.

It wasn't Morgina with whom she made contact, but Sharayah, who was earlier and more enigmatic, at least to me. She seemed to live in far less interesting times, in the supposed Chinese sense of the term. She was free; she wasn't imprisoned, like the prime template that she had yet to become. She had a lover, and an abundant supply of blood to feed her hunger and ecstasy.

It was, as always, dark. Sharayah was in the principal harbor of Atlantis, about to board a ship. The sailing ships of Atlantis seemed to me to be more akin to coasters than long-distance sailing ships, although I'm no expert on naval architecture, but they were considerably larger than the Arab dhows that seemed to inherit their design. They sometimes carried passengers all the way to the Atlantean colony of Clarica on the west African coast, and they often set sail by night if the tides and winds were favorable.

Time was collapsed in Sheena's narrative; while mere minutes were passing in Harehills Lane, hours were going by in Atlantis.

Sharayah was bound for the Clarican city of Avra. She was excited, because she had never gone that far from the Atlantean mainland before, and slightly frightened by the awful silence of the sea. The night was bright enough when the boat set sail, but the sky soon darkened as clouds gathered, overtaking the craft because the wind blew faster at altitude. It began to rain, but it wasn't a storm, and Sharayah didn't take shelter down below. The raindrops weren't cold, and they fell with an eerie gentleness, like sentimental tears—not tears of grief, Sheena told me, but the kind you shed at the end of a film when lovers are reunited after an interval of heartrending separation and danger.

Below decks, some of Sharayah's fellow passengers began to sing, as if to shut out the rain and the loneliness, but Sharayah and Sheena resisted the inevitable temptation to join in, because Sharayah wanted to savor the rain and Sheena had already explained why she couldn't sing me the songs of lost Atlantis. When Sharayah opened her mouth to take in the falling drops, she found it strangely sweet, almost as if there were a trace of blood in every slowly descending drop....

In Harehills Lane, Sheena and I were touching all the while, caressing one another, slowly and unhurriedly. We were perfectly relaxed, although we weren't drowsy, in spite of the lateness of the hour. If I had set my mind to the serious business of invention, I would have had to concentrate harder, but that obligation had released its hold of late.

I wasn't entranced, and I wasn't drifting off to sleep....

But for the first time, I remembered.

I really and truly remembered, with a certainty that would have instantly dismissed all doubts and confusions arising from the knowledge that there had, after all, never been any such place as Atlantis, had any such dismissal been necessary.

As it happened, though, I didn't remember being in Atlantis proper, or any of its satellite island states. I wasn't with Sharayah on her ship, tasting the rain, and I wasn't in the capital, plotting some ingenious scheme to get through to Morgina in spite of all the guards and precautions surrounding her.

What I remembered was being on a tiny island, not much larger than a sandbar. The interior was covered with thorn-laden scrub, interrupted by a few scrawny date-palms, but I'd already stripped the trees of their unripe fruit—at considerable cost to the integrity of my skin, which was scored all over with streaky scabs.

I'd managed to squeeze a little moisture from leaves and a few inedible fruits, but there was no gentle rain to supply me with fresh water and I was fearfully thirsty. I was lying on the thin strip of sand that separated the scrub from the breaking waves, and would certainly have been unconscious had it not been for the torment of my thirst, because I was very weak.

My eyes were open and I was staring up at the sky, desperately wishing that the clouds obscuring the stars would break, although I rolled my head from side to side occasionally, hoping that I might glimpse the lanterns of a passing ship.

I didn't said a word to Sheena. I was too startled, and too amazed. I feared that if I spoke, I might break the spell, and I didn't want the experience to evaporate like a dream. I wanted to examine every detail of the apparent memory, and the fact that it was painful only made it more fascinating, more intriguing.

If I gave any indication at all to Sheena that I had been transported, it could only have been my body language that conveyed the hint. I said nothing—but I think she knew. Or maybe it was Sharayah who knew, or even Morgina , in spite of living in the future of the time I thought I was remembering—she was, after all, the prime template of which Sharayah was somehow only a copy. One way or another, the tale that Sheena was spinning hypnotically changed, seamlessly, into an account of an errand of mercy.

"The ship is too slow," Sheena/Sharayah reported. "It'll never get there in time, and I know it. I can't go below to join in with the singing. I have to use magic. It's dangerous, but it's the only way. I have to fly, no matter what the risk or the cost.

"It's very difficult, to sing my own song when I can still hear the other being sung, but it has to be done, and the sound of the rain on the sea helps me. I'm beginning to sing my spell, silently, although I can't repeat it aloud, and I know it's going to work, even though I've never sung such a spell before, because the need is so great.

"I'm singing the spell, silently, and I'm taking wing from the deck of the ship. I'm flying so fast that I'm out of the shadow of the rain clouds within minutes, although I can see darkness on the horizon again almost as soon as the moonlight touches me. The clouds on the horizon are different, high and cold, remote and uncaring, but they don't matter."

Meanwhile, I couldn't remember my name, but I didn't think of that as strange, I was in dire straits, and names didn't matter. Only thirst mattered, and the possibility of relief. I knew that I had known, once, exactly who I was and where I was bound and how I'd come to be marooned on that tiny strip of land somewhere between Atlantis and Africa, but all of that had been driven deep into my mind, to leave the surface of my thoughts free for desperation and hope.

In another world, the hope would have died, and in due course the desperation would have died too as I shriveled into a desiccated corpse, silver-grey upon the amber sand, fading by slow degrees to whiteness. But the era I was remembering was an age of magic and miracles, and there was no need to die.

A winged shadow fell out of the soulless night, and metamorphosed into a human female. I had no idea who she was, and could not have recognized her had I known her name. There were no mirrors in Atlantis; for all the magic that Sharayah and Morgina had, and all their skill in description, they could not describe their own faces, and Sheena had never seen them. Sheena had no idea what her past selves looked like, but they couldn't have looked like her. If they had, even though I wasn't myself, even though I was remembering someone completely different, I would surely have recognized her. Wouldn't I?

Sharayah was small and slender, and the pale features of her black-framed face were so perfect that I wished I could see their true colors. But I was also seized by a premonition that something was wrong, that my need had demanded something from her that was more than she had to give, no matter how clever or willing she might be to offer it.

She had no water, but she cut her left breast beneath the nipple, and gave me blood to drink. The blood was sweeter and more intoxicating than wine, and it quenched my dreadful thirst, if only for a little while.

Having done that, my savior sank down beside me on the sand, utterly exhausted, and began to caress me with her fingers, and what had been memory faded by slow degrees into a dream, which extended, in the way dreams sometimes do, rendering time elastic, so that the night went on forever...or would have done, had forever been a possibility.

Perhaps forever was possible, on that island, adrift in eternity. Perhaps forever is not only possible but inevitable, if you can look at the world from the right point of view. But when the memory faded away, I had nowhere else to go but the mundane flat of which I'd inherited a third from my father, where forever was no more possible for me than it had been for him.

So forever wasn't a possibility for me, once I awoke, and the dream had always been faded, as dreams always are, like a photocopy of a photocopy, lacking the immediacy of reality. It evaporated, as did the darkness of the night.

The unknown woman tried to pull away then, but I caught and held her.

*Stay*, I said, insistently but not aloud—and she consented to be held, while the sun rose and the dark world filled with color.

Newton only pretended that there are seven colors in our rainbow because he thought that seven was the appropriate number. In fact, there are five: red, yellow, green, blue and violet—but Newton must have remembered fragments of past lives spent in imaginary histories, consciously or unconsciously, and must have known that there really were seven colors in the rainbows that shone in Atlantean skies. Two of them have been lost, and no longer have names, but I know now that they lay beyond red and violet, not within the spectrum that extends from red to violet, like Newton's invented colors.

The color of the sun was yellow, and the sea was blue. The date palms and the thorn-bushes were green—but the unknown woman's face and costume were tinted with colors I had never seen before. I know now that we only think that blood is red because we've lost the ability to see the other color with which the red is mingled, just as we've lost the ability to taste blood as vampires taste it, and to draw that special nourishment from it for which vampires ceaselessly thirst.

Had I drunk more frequently or more abundantly of Sheena's blood, my remembered self might have been more vampire than I was when the sun rose on that tiny island, forgotten even though it lay within the boundaries of the empire of Lost Atlantis. Alas, I remained far too human, then and now. My remembered self wasn't a hero. He wasn't a knight errant who could have reached out through time, and defied all the three-dimensional precautions surrounding Morgina simply by using a fourth. He hadn't thought of that, any more than I had—but he had an excuse, because he was living in the past, and didn't even know that Morgina existed, let alone that she was the key to everything, including the mysterious magical bird-woman who had just saved his life with her blood and a silent song.

As soon as the light hit the unknown woman—who was surely Sharayah, although I couldn't recognize her—she began to dissolve. That part of the mythology of trashy novels was true after all, at least in Atlantis, in spite of Sheena's understandable skepticism.

I felt a terrible sense of betrayal, because I too had always believed that vampires shouldn't dissolve in sunlight, because that was an aspect of the myth that was mere historians' slander, but I stifled my scream when she tried to speak. I needed to hear what she was saying, even though her voice had already decayed to the merest whisper.

"The spell was too costly," she told me. "But nothing really dies, and nothing changes its inmost nature. Don't be afraid. I'll return with the night, and you won't go thirsty, no matter how long you remain here."

I was already awake by the time the whisper concluded, as far away as far away could be from any mere dream, but it wasn't until I opened my eyes that I found Sheena dead.

# XIV

I was hysterical, of course, but I think I managed to do all the things you were supposed to do back in 1999, in the right order. I phoned an ambulance, and then I set about trying to resuscitate her. I breathed air into her lungs and I pummeled her chest, until the paramedics from St James's arrived and took over.

It was only after their arrival that I actually lost control. I remember shouting: "She's only nineteen fucking years old, for fuck's sake—how the fuck can she have a fucking heart attack?" but I don't think the paramedics held the unnecessary expletives against me. That wasn't why they wouldn't let me accompany the corpse to the hospital.

I was sufficiently coherent, in any case, to give them the address and phone number of her official next of kin, so that they could send someone else to deliver the terrible news.

I couldn't stay in the flat, and I certainly couldn't face Mrs. Howell and Libby, so I started walking eastwards, towards the rising sun, and I continued until I reached the urban wilderness of Whitkirk. Perhaps it was the coincidence of rhymes that drew me there; perhaps I thought the name was magical, and summoning me. I wasn't in my right mind, so that could have been the case—but because I wasn't in my right mind, my memory of what happened is blurred and disconnected. In the early hours, while Sheena was entranced, time in Atlantis had been passing much more rapidly than time in Leeds, but now it was time in Leeds that seemed to be flying, and sometimes vanishing without bothering to elapse.

Davy was already up and about, busy with noise. I leaned on the doorbell until it penetrated the wall of sound. When he opened the door he seemed angry, but as soon as he saw me the anger metamorphosed into something else—something essentially unfathomable.

"Is she...?" he asked, but couldn't force the final word past his lips.

"This might be a good time to rip my head off," I told him, in a white fury. "You seem to have got to the head of the queue—but then, you always knew that you would, didn't you?"

"It wasn't your fault," he said, standing aside to let me in, and then closing the door to exclude the world from our private business. "However it happened, it wasn't your fault."

"If you weren't so much bigger than me," I told him, "I'd be seriously considering the possibility of ripping *your* head off. I must have been blind and stupid not to see it. First you, then her sister, even Trudi, of all people. I thought it was just run-of-the-mill protectiveness. Even when Libby practically spelled it out in letters of fire, telling me in so many words that there was something I didn't know, it didn't click. But you knew, didn't you? Whatever the big secret was, you were in on it and I wasn't."

"Libby would have told you eventually," he said, plaintively. "I thought she would have told you ages ago, in fact. But I couldn't—she swore me to secrecy. It wasn't for me to tell you; it was for her. She must have intended do...she told me, after all. When the time...she obviously didn't expect...I'm sorry, okay...I didn't know...so soon."

The message was clear, even though the sentences weren't complete. They hadn't expected it to happen so soon—but they *had* expected it. Libby would have told me eventually, but...why hadn't she? Perhaps because she wanted to be absolutely sure that it was serious first. Perhaps she wanted to convince herself, as far as it was possible, that I was man enough to handle it.

I could understand that. The only thing I didn't understand, at that moment in time, but desperately needed to know, was why Sheena had been part of the conspiracy of silence. She had known me through and through, even if her sister and her ex-boyfriend hadn't.

And then I did understand. She hadn't told me because she didn't know. Libby hadn't told her either. Libby knew, and Mrs. Howell knew, but Sheena didn't. They hadn't told her that the sword of Damocles was hanging over her head. They were protecting her. Perhaps they even thought they were protecting her by not telling me, even though—or perhaps because—they had told Davy.

"So tell me," I said to Big Bad Davy, when I was a little bit calmer—although not much, admittedly—"exactly how it comes about that a nineteen-year-old girl can have a heart attack, just like that."

Davy sighed. "Do you know what protein C is?" he asked.

"No," I answered, sourly. "I'm only a fucking sociology graduate."

"It's one of the clotting factors in the blood. Do you know what homeostasis is?"

"Feedback," I said. "Like a thermostat. If you're talking about people, it's the control mechanism that regulates body temperature. You get too cold, you shiver to generate heat. You get too hot, you sweat to lose it."

"It's not just temperature," he told me. "All kinds of bodily processes have to be regulated by chemical feedback systems. Blood clotting is one of them. If blood doesn't clot readily enough, you can bleed to death from a trivial cut. If it clots too readily, clots form even when there isn't any damage, and they get stuck—usually in the capillaries in the legs, but sometimes in more dangerous places. A clot in the brain can cause a stroke; a clot in a heart-valve can cause heart failure. Nowadays, doctors can treat conditions like hemophilia with clotting factors like thrombin and protein C, and conditions of the opposite kind with warfarin and hirudin, but Sheena's condition wasn't amenable to any kind of continuous therapy. They didn't even know it existed until fifteen years ago or thereabouts. Her father was one of the first people to be properly diagnosed—posthumously, unfortunately."

"How can you have both problems?" I demanded. "It doesn't make sense."

"The level of protein C in the blood is controlled by a feedback mechanism," he said. "Unfortunately, Sheena's father had a bad gene, which made a faulty version of the enzyme that's supposed to switch off protein C production when it reaches the right level. It wasn't that the mechanism didn't work at all—just that it was dodgy. Sometimes, his levels went way up, and sometimes they went way down. His children had a fifty-fifty chance of inheriting the dodgy gene, and that's the way it worked out. Libby was clear, Sheena wasn't. They didn't actually have a test for the gene until a couple of years ago, when they finally managed to locate it, but the symptoms were pretty obvious. Given two or three more years of the Human Genome Project, they'll probably be able to sequence the protein and identify the fault in the dodgy version, and that might open up at least the possibility of finding an effective treatment, but at the time Mrs. Howell and Libby got the diagnosis there was nothing that could be done except treat Sheena's symptoms as and when they appeared, according to type, so...."

"So they decided not to tell her," I finished for him, as enlightenment dawned in the deadly fashion of an Atlantean dawn. "Because they didn't want her to know that she was living under a death sentence." And then, following the logic I'd already glimpsed, I said: "Is that why you broke up with her, you bastard? Is that why Libby hesitated over telling me?"

"No!" he said. "At least, not in the way you think. Okay, I admit, it made a difference when Libby told me. I got scared. Look at me! I'm twice her size. I'd always felt like I was handling precious porcelain—how do you think it made me feel when I was told that a bad bruise could kill her? Maybe I did overdo the carefulness, and maybe she did begin to wonder whether I might be going off her, but that wasn't it. It wasn't. We just weren't right, except for the music, because I could never share her fantasies, could never commit myself to that part of her life…and I knew that if she didn't have time to spare, she shouldn't have to spend it *making do*. I didn't dump her. We just…fell apart."

Maybe it was self-justificatory bullshit and maybe it wasn't, but that didn't matter. It had been the right result, after all. Sheena didn't have the time to spare, and she shouldn't have had spend it pretending to make love to Davy just because she made music with him. She needed to be free of him, so that she could find me.

Unlike Sheena and Davy, Sheena and I *had* been right. If anything were ever meant to be, we'd have been one of the things that was meant to be—but whether we live a million lifetimes or one, nothing is ever really *meant to be*. What isn't pure chance is what you make of the cards you're dealt, and Sheena and I had made the most of each other since chance had thrown us together.

We hadn't finished our journey, but we were on the way, with the heading set, and we were together, bound in a way that she could never have been bound with Davy, or anyone else. No one could have made any more of either of us, in the limited time we'd had, than we'd made of one another, and there was no use complaining about the unfairness of the ill luck that had torn us apart. It hadn't been cruel fate, or any god that any human being had ever believed in. Life never had been morally ordered, even in Atlantis or Arcadia; it had just been a roll of the dice, just a matter of hazard, as it still was.

I couldn't blame Davy. I certainly couldn't hold it against him that he hadn't told me what Libby and Mrs. Howell wouldn't, and I couldn't even rail at him for not having told Sheena—because I knew that even if she hadn't heard the ugly clinical details, Sheena had known everything she actually needed to know. She'd always known, even if she'd never raised it to the level of consciousness or connected it to her absent father's premature demise, that she was living in mortal danger. Why else would she have been so implacably determined to get in touch with her past selves, to cram a thousand lifetimes into one horribly narrow span?

I had helped. I had to cling to that. I had helped.

The funeral was absolute hell. The church service was all completely false. The vicar made a speech, but it was all boilerplate, repeated in his clerical equivalent of a telephone voice, and he insisted on calling her Susan, so he was talking about someone else entirely. Libby said "a few words," as the conventional phrase has it, but she called her Susan too, even though she had been instrumental in helping her become Sheena, and she didn't say a word about anything that had meant anything to Sheena. Mrs. Howell was no more capable of saying a few words than I was, but Trudi Hemming made a short speech on behalf of all the staff of the call center, also in her telephone voice, as absent herself as Sheena was from what she said. It was a complete farce.

It was even worse at the house, afterwards. Libby and her mother kept giving me books, pictures, CDs and tapes that Sheena had never bothered transferring from the house to the flat, saying: "I think she'd have wanted you to have these." She probably would have, but that didn't make it any easier standing beside a chair piled high with the obscene loot of her brief life. Davy had already given me a dozen spare tapes and had promised me faithfully that when the CD finally came off the presses I'd get the very first copy. On the other hand, I certainly wasn't going to turn anything down that had anything of Sheena in it, even a second-hand paperback whose pages had once been turned by her black-painted fingernails.

I couldn't eat anything and the tea was vile as well as weak. It wouldn't have tasted any better even if I hadn't still been nursing the remains of the previous night's hangover.

Libby tried to explain, of course, although by that time, it was quite unnecessary.

"I really was going to tell you," she said. "I was going to tell you weeks ago, in fact, but Suzy seemed so happy, and I didn't want to risk disturbing that. It wasn't that I was afraid that you'd break up with her, or that your attitude would change, the way Davy's had—he wasn't right for her anyway, and I could tell that. It was just that…well, she was so *happy*."

"Her name," I said, "is Sheena. I understand why she had to be Susan in the church, but we're back in the real world now. Her name is Sheena."

She didn't correct my use of the present tense. She was evidently uncomfortable in my company, so I didn't force it upon her for long. I didn't force it on anyone for long, once I'd given Mrs. Howell my condolences, and she'd given me hers. She didn't try to explain. She didn't even think there was anything to explain. It had never occurred to her that she might tip me off that I had fallen in love with someone who might drop dead at any minute. She had her own old-fashioned ideas about the demands of discretion.

Lily was waiting for me in the flat when I got home. As co-owner, she had a spare key and a sense of entitlement. She'd tidied up while I was out, but at least she'd persuaded Mum to stay at home, so I didn't have to listen to any complaints about the inadequacy of the vacuum cleaner and the lack of an ironing board.

"How do you feel?" she asked.

"Like shit," I told her.

"It must have been difficult."

"It was a farce."

She had already offered me a shoulder to cry on, and I'd turned it down. She was tacitly offering again, because she couldn't believe I didn't need one—and she might have been right, but there was no way I was going to take my little sister into my confidence about any of the private stuff that had gone on between Sheena and me. I wasn't going to talk to her about the sex, about Atlantis, about vampirism, or about how I felt, beyond the observation that it was shitty. I was operating on a need to know basis. I had to. The only shoulder I had any intention of crying on was Sheena's, which wouldn't be there in the flesh, alas, but would be easy enough to imagine…impossible in fact, not to imagine, once darkness fell and I was alone, in Leeds or Atlantis or anywhere else in the wilderness of spacetime.

Not that Lily had any intention of leaving me alone, while she didn't have any urgent requirement to be elsewhere, nor had she any intention of leaving the slightest platitude unvoiced, while she still had breath to spare—but it wasn't her fault. She was seventeen. She was following what she thought was the script. She was even doing psychology A-level, which gave her the illusion of an insight she couldn't possibly have. She wanted to protect me, with all the resources at her disposal. It required an effort on my part to weather her sympathy and her primitive counseling kindly—but the effort probably did me good, and I was grateful for the fact that her heart was in the right place. If she hadn't been eager to pester me, it would have hurt my feelings more than anything she could actually say. Eventually, I got rid of her, in the kindest fashion I could contrive.

After hell and Atlantis, it was back to purgatory again when I turned up for work the day after the funeral for the early evening shift. A dreadful hush seemed to have descended on the call center, and the muted ringing tones of the multitudinous phones were transmuted by the lack of competition into a sinister symphony. I got seven invitations to go out with the girls when the shift ended, and seven assurances that they'd behave themselves like perfect ladies if I did.

I believed them. They'd have sat quietly in a corner, with me in the middle, sipping their drinks with all due decorum, offering their counsel and their sympathy with less cod psychology than Lily, but similar sincerity. Although some of them, at least, including pretty Rachel and sweet Maxine, would probably have made themselves available, in case I needed further consolation of a more physical variety, they would have done so with unprecedented discretion and sensitivity.

I said no seven times, very politely. Only five of them, including Rachel and Maxine, went on to say, "Well, if you ever need to talk...."

I didn't. For the time being, I needed to listen.

I played the tapes over and over, and when Davy eventually arrived to make me a present of the newly cut CD—from which *Graveyard Love* had been sensitively omitted, although the Byronic kiss and sting were still there—I played it over and over and over.

I wanted to be free of myself, but hearing Sheena sing those words, far less plaintively than seemed warranted, didn't do the trick. I wasn't free, especially of myself, even though my true self was invisible. Every time I looked into a mirror, I saw nothing but emptiness.

Davy told me that the songs on the CD were the best of Sheena's work as well as the best of his, but they weren't. They weren't even the rest of her work, left over when body and soul had fled, because I knew full well—although I could hardly confide the truth to anyone else—that her soul hadn't fled at all.

Sheena was a vampire, and a magicienne, and she knew perfectly well how to exist in a disembodied state. She was in no hurry to be reincarnated, because she understood well enough how much future remained to the universal soul for serial refragmentation. The Earth had existed for four billion years, while humankind had been around for a mere million; the planet would exist for four billion more, and humankind had a better than even chance of seeing far more than a million of that, albeit significantly transmogrified, provided that the next falling asteroid was no bigger than the one that had finally drowned the last remnants of Atlantis and scoured its fugitive relics from the jagged residue of the mid-Atlantic ridge.

Sheena wasn't in any rush to explore flesh again for her own sake, and she knew that I needed her to linger. If she had really wanted to be free of herself when she wrote that song, as I assumed that she really had, she didn't want it any longer. She had met me in the interim. Now, she wanted to kiss and sting in an emergent world, reeking and damp from out of the slime. Now, she had a reason to remain, suspended between death and life. She was bound by blood, symbolically and literally, and she had a source, offered freely, as it had to be in order to nourish her soul.

I played the songs over and over, regardless of the fact that their message was out of date, because I knew that music is the purest magic of all as well as the greatest mystery, and I needed magic. I needed to go way beyond common sense, into the supernatural. I needed the music to take everything out of me that wasn't just waste, because there was so much in me that was just waste, and I couldn't bear it.

Sheena had been right when she told me that the only way to get a true appreciation of what it means to be alive is to have died a thousand times, and I knew that I didn't yet have that true appreciation. She had been right to tell me that until I'd lived and lost a million joyful moments, I wouldn't realize how precious they were. And above all, she was right to tell me that once I'd had the even briefest glimpse of other worlds, this one would never be enough.

I knew that I only had to attract the right kind of night visitor, and feed her, to make the connection I needed in the fullness of time, eventually to find the muse who would teach me the art of living in a shattered and shambolic world, who would allow me to create myself anew. Every night, I cut myself over the heart with a razor blade, eventually drawing a labyrinth of neatly curved lines, in order that Sheena could feed. It wasn't strictly necessary, given that she could install herself readily enough within the chambers of my heart, but I wanted her beside me as well as inside me. I wanted to make an offering, an honest libation.

I always had to wipe the remaining blood away with cotton wool, because I couldn't lick my own heart, being bound by the limits of physical practicality, but that didn't matter. It wasn't as if I were a vampire cast away on some desert island, driven to desperate measures in the hope of sustaining myself until rescue came, if it ever did. In any case, any nourishment that it provided for me would have been exceedingly meager by comparison with the need it filled in her. For her, vampirism had never been a matter of sinking pints the way lads sup ale, and now it was even more refined than it had been when she had been incarnate, but also more avid. Now, she could leech the blood out of my veins, the marrow out of my bones, the elixir of life out of my very soul, without requiring the delicate touch of her purple-stained lips or the hypnotic gaze of her neutron-star eyes—but she needed the gift, the demonstration of my love, my permanent commitment.

I tried my utmost to remember Atlantis and Arcadia, or even to dream about them, but it was exceedingly difficult. I could have made things up, of course, but I didn't want to do that. Fiction is all about contriving happy endings in a world where the only real endings are fire and the grave, but real comfort has to be found and not contrived, and if the supernatural is the only place where real comfort can be found, that's where you have to look for it. If you also find nightmares there, that's the price you have to pay.

I paid it.

The truth is that you can't just *make things up*—not in the final analysis. In the short term, deliberate invention can function as a mnemonic device, helping you to get in touch with the unconscious, to ease yourself into the knack of breaking through to the unconscious, and to authentic reality, but that's really a game for two players. When you're on your own, without a teacher and a partner, without significant assistance, you can't just make things up, even as a cunning stratagem. I couldn't, anyhow. I still can't. You have to find what you need, even if that makes you a puppet in the hands of your own creation.

I knew where to look. I knew how. I paid the price. But I couldn't remember. I couldn't even dream. I had to be content with cutting myself, and watching the blood stain the cotton wool, clotting with minutely judged alacrity, neither too quickly nor too slowly.

There was always time for Sheena to drink her fill, and she never took too much. She knew the value of extravagance, but she knew the value of economy too. Her spirit had none of the inbuilt irresponsibility of her body and her blood. She was a vampire—and how!

I talked to her, of course. Oh, how I talked! But I didn't talk about Atlantis or Arcadia, because she no longer needed my help to recall her past lives. The wandering soul remembers everything. Even Plato, who really didn't know the first thing about Atlantis, knew that. I talked to her about the future, because the future was unmade, and the future was where we'd meet again, if we ever did.

"In the future," I told her, "all things are possible. In the future, our descendants will learn to see those two lost colors all over again, and they'll find out how to sing again, in all the languages that ever were or ever will be, in true harmony. It won't always be like that, of course, because the course of progress never runs smoothly, and there'll be dark days when civilization all but vanishes and even vampires starve, but as long as the sun shines there'll be new dawns, and because light sustains life it also, in the ultimate analysis, sustains all the forms of undeath, even the photophobic ones.

"In time, of course, the sun will begin to fade, reddening as it ages, always reaching for that other color, which is the better part of the color of blood. In the end, that color will be all that's left, and even that will fade as the sun shrinks and dies, until there's nothing left of it but the black hole at its core and a surrounding chaos of strange energies. With luck, my love, you'll survive even that; in four billion years the descendants of humans ought to be able to reach the stars, and the undead will surely lead the way."

She didn't answer, but I didn't really expect her to. After all, her voice was the one part of her that I still had in superabundance, and it was always there, filling the space between me and the walls.

I want to be free, of myself, of myself.

I want to be free, of myself.

I didn't really need her voice, although I was very glad to have it, and in such abundance. In the final analysis, I only needed her thirst. It would surely have been better if I'd been able to remember, or even to dream, but life isn't fair, and you have to play the cards you're dealt to the best of your ability. All I could give her was blood, and for that, she wasn't obliged to be a generous Muse.

But still, I had her thirst.

I knew she was there every time I cut myself. She was there the rest of the time too, day and night. She was with me when I slept, no matter how dark and bleak my dreaming was, and she was with me when I went to work, to play the puppet in my best telephone manner, always speaking softly and always following the script with minute precision. She was with me in the Headrow and Harehills Lane, at the Merrion Centre and Elland Road... but when I cut myself, I knew she was there, because I knew exactly how thirsty she was, and exactly what she needed to satisfy her thirst.

She'd have done as much for me, if the situation had somehow been reversed, although I'm not sure that I could have done as much for her, in my disembodied state. I was such an incompetent vampire, such an incompetent dreamer, such an incompetent rememberer, afflicted with the everyday dementia that only allows the past to filter through in strange fugitive flashes wrenched out of context, superimposed by the imagination over the blurred reality that defective eyes can no longer perceive accurately.

Even though I would have been incompetent as a disembodied vampire, though, I couldn't help wishing, sometimes, that I was dead and Sheena was still alive. There was so much more she might have been able to get out of incarnate life, if she'd had a little more of it.

"Not without you," I sometimes imagined her saying, when I followed that train of thought—but I had to stop following it then, because it would ultimately have led me to thinking that if we couldn't be together alive, maybe it would be better to be together dead, and that was the very last thing she wanted. She wanted me alive, so that she could fed herself in my blood, so that she could sustain her vampiric reality with my symbolic blood. Dead, she needed me even more than she had needed me alive. No matter how dreary life was, with the saving exception of her presence, I had to hang on to it, not to enable her presence to exist, because she was immortal, but to give her an anchorage, a perpetual source of vital force, an elixir of love.

In other lives, of course, she still had the joys of incarnation, even if they were sometimes frustrated and tarnished, like Morgina's, because everything is everpresent in the timelessness of the universal soul, and there are undoubted rewards, too, in being free to drift upon the tides of time, in a disembodied state, incapable for a little while of anything but drifting. For the time being, though, she was with me, and she would stay with me for as long as I wanted her to stay, for as long as I needed her to stay, because we were bound, united. I didn't have to lose her a second time around, and I didn't.

I clung on, and I clung hard.

# XV

The more blood I shed, and the more of it that Sheena consumed, the greater the change in me became, but I didn't become the kind of vampire she had been. She had never promised me that. All she had ever promised me was that I would be changed, and changed forever, and I was.

In a way, it might have been easier to become a shadow of my former self, simply to pine away, as if to die of a broken heart; but I didn't have a broken heart. My heart was healthy—a fit abode even for the sickliest of disembodied vampire spirits—and I didn't want to be a shadow while I still had blood to feed a shadow's thirst.

Sheena had needed me while she was alive, because nobody else could give her what she needed then, and she needed me just as much now that she was dead, because mine was the blood to which she had committed herself, willingly and desirously. When her body had been more than ash and dust it had been my body that she had needed to give her comfort, and now that there was nothing left of her flesh but ash and dust it was my blood that her vampire spirit needed for comfort. Any body might have done for warmth, and any blood might have slaked her thirst, but for true comfort and true fulfillment, it had to be my blood, exactly as it had previously had to be my body. I offered that blood, as a testament of love.

It was for comfort, too, as well as for true fulfillment, that I needed her. For me, nobody else would have sufficed, even for warmth—but what I needed most urgently and most ardently was her comfort. That was why I cut myself, night after night after night, to feed her and to try—crudely and hopelessly—to feed myself. She was always satisfied, but I never was. I continued to thirst, because no matter how much I had changed, I wasn't the kind of vampire who could sustain myself on a desert island, with none but a ghostly spirit for company.

"Diseases can only produced diseased dreams," Sheena had said to me once, in reply to some flippant remark I'd made, when I was playing the game lightly,  not realizing how much more important it was than life and death. She was probably right about syphilis, which was what I'd had in mind, but she was wrong about her own disease. Out of the sickness of trees, beautiful orchids can grow, and from her defective genome, something ineffably beautiful and incredibly true had germinated and blossomed. It had been a unique and wonderful privilege to be admitted to it, to be gifted with it.

Some people might reckon me to be a trifle sick, but they don't know. They really don't know, and I really don't appreciate all the efforts they've made over the years to "help me recover," although I forgive them, because they mean well.

"Life goes on, love," said Mum, more than once—and she was absolutely right. She had no idea how right she was: life does go on, but that doesn't mean that it shouldn't hurt.

"It could have been either of us," Libby Howell told me, once, when she came to the flat to see how I was doing. "It could have been both, or neither. It could have been me and not her. Maybe it should have been. I was the older one, after all, I had the right of the first-born to the inheritance. If I said I wished I could trade places with her, I'd be a liar, but maybe that's the way it should have been."

"No," I said, in my best telephone manner. "It shouldn't. You couldn't have handled it the way Sheena handled it."

"We never even talked about it," she went on. "That was absolutely the worst thing about not telling her. We could never talk about it, because she didn't know. It's almost as if we weren't sisters at all. I talked about it to Tru, but never to her. Tru did her best to be kind, but…well, you know how difficult she finds it. I'm really sorry that I couldn't talk to Suzy."

"It doesn't matter," I assured her. "Sheena knew what she needed to know. She said what she needed to say. She heard what she needed to hear."

"From you. What did I ever give her, apart from that stupid name?"

"It was what she needed. If it hadn't been, she wouldn't have taken it."

I think Libby went away, on that occasion, feeling a little better, glad that we'd shared a few confidences. Perhaps she would have genuinely pleased that I was bearing up and doing well, although I'm not at all sure that she took away that impression. She didn't offer me any more than her good wishes, because she was being loyal to her little sister. She knew, deep down, even though she'd never be able to say so, that Sheena wasn't entirely gone. She might even have known what Sheena was, even though she couldn't actually believe in ghosts, let alone in vampires. Working in Gap and living at home had fixated her mind on superficial things. Her mother was like my mother, full of common sense and well-tried saws. I never heard Mrs. Howell say "life goes on, love," but I expect she did, even when there was no one in the room to hear her…perhaps especially then.

The first person to see my scars—inevitably, I suppose—was Mum, but she didn't see them for what they were. "What have you been doing, love?" she asked. I could have told her that I'd been out collecting blackberries and she'd have believed it, but what I actually said was a more blatant lie, even though it was nearer to the truth.

"I've had them for ages," I said. "They'll be fine, as long as I never get scurvy. Collagen dissolves when you get scurvy, apparently, and the wounds open up."

"You and your books," she said—which was a tamer version of "fucking sociology graduate." I kept drinking the orange juice, though. I didn't want to start coming apart at the seams.

They say that time heals, but it doesn't. At best, time scars, and there's no orange juice for the soul that will keep you safe from those occasional moments of spiritual scurvy when the scars break down and everything pours out. Even though I couldn't remember, or even dream, I still had those nightmare moments when everything seemed to fall apart and it felt as if all the blood was flooding out of me at once, incapable of clotting, inviting every supernatural carrion-drinker for miles to fall upon me like a flock of vampire crows. The flock was sometimes so dense that my own guardian vampire had no chance to defend her territory—but such moments did pass as my spiritual clotting factors cut in, never more than a little too late.

I always got through the night, ready to return to puppet life in Phoneland, where even the harpies still treated me with kid gloves, and the gorgon, when she occasionally deigned to glance in my direction, looked at me with naked pity.

"Actually," I confided to Jez one night in the Countess of Cromartie, when I finally allowed him to bully me into letting him buy me a pint of bitter, "life doesn't go on. Only death goes on. We begin to die as soon as we begin to live. It's death that whittles the embryo into human shape, death that clears out all the cellular compost day by day, as life takes its inevitable toll. Life doesn't go on at all—it just flows away, bit by bit, emptying us out, even if we were never really full."

"Yeah," he said, wisely, although he didn't understand a word I'd said, for the sake of humoring me. "Too bloody right. That's why you have to make the most of what you've got. Fight it, mate. You might lose, but you have to fight." He couldn't see that that was exactly what I was doing, far more cleverly than he could know. At least he had the grace to refrain from making observations about the number of pebbles on the beach or fish in the sea. He'd been out with the girls too many times to be under any delusions about any fuck being a good fuck. He didn't know enough to envy me what I now had, but he knew enough to envy me what I'd had before.

"She was a grand lass, Sheena,' he said. "A bit strange, but who can blame her? We take our health too much for granted."

"Yes, she was," I said. "And yes, we do. Do you mind if I don't get another round in—no offence, but I think I'd rather be at home."

"No, mate," he said. "Another time, eh?"

"Another time," I echoed. That was where was I headed, although I didn't expect to get there that night, or any time soon.

The next day I was on a late shift, so I had a long lie-in. Mercifully, though, I was up and dressed and not looking like death warmed up when the doorbell rang.

It was Trudi Hemming. I was amazed. She's hardly addressed two words to me since the funeral, and I'd got the distinct impression that she was avoiding me like the plague, even though she was the one who had declared that we were friends.

I invited her in and made us a cup of tea.

"To what do I owe the pleasure?" I asked.

"I owe you an apology," she said.

"For what?"

"For not telling you about Sheena."

"You couldn't," I reminded her. "Libby had sworn you to secrecy. You couldn't say anything to anyone, including Sheena."

"I owe her an apology too, although it's too late to give it to her. I'm not the kind of person who can be relied on to keep promises. I could have broken it. So, yes, I owe you an apology. I can't help feeling slightly responsible."

"That's ridiculous," I said. "There was nothing you or anyone could have done to prevent her from dying."

"Not that," she said. "For you and her. I could have prevented that, but I didn't. Quite the contrary."

"No you couldn't," I insisted, but couldn't help my curiosity taking over and adding: "How?"

"If I'd fucked you that first night, after the Black Boar. Everything from then on would have been different. She wouldn't have touched you with a bargepole, if I'd told her you'd fucked me."

I was amazed. "That's ridiculous on so many counts," I marveled.

"Really? Are you saying that if I'd handled things differently, that if I'd actually gone out of my way to tempt you instead of putting you off, you wouldn't have fucked me? Can you honestly say that?"

I couldn't honestly say that, so I didn't try. "It wouldn't have made any difference," I said. "It wouldn't have made any difference what you'd said about me afterwards, either. Sheena and I were made for one another. Nothing could have kept us apart."

"If you say so," she said, feigning contempt. I got the impression that it was exactly what she'd wanted me to say—that in some perverse fashion, she'd wanted the reassurance. "But I did encourage it. I told you you'd be good for her, and I think you were. I didn't tell you that it wouldn't work out so well for you. I know you're just a prick, but even so…an apology is in order."

"I was good for her," I said. "If you really had helped to bring us together, you'd only have reason to congratulate yourself. And it was better than good for me. No apology necessary. If I really thought you had anything to do with it, I'd be down on my knees kissing your feet in gratitude."

"Don't do that," she said. "Been there, done that, got the T-shirt—and drool between my toes." She paused.

I knew that the apology, as fake as it was unnecessary, couldn't be the reason she had come round; that it was just an inept ice-breaker. I didn't think I'd ever told her my address, and didn't think that Sheena would have told her either, but while delving for a hypothesis as to what I really owed the dubious pleasure, I came up with a suspicion.

"Did Libby Howell ask you to come and see me?" I asked.

She seemed genuinely surprised. "No," she said. "Why would she?"

"I don't know," I said. "I was just trying to figure out why you're here. I can't believe it was to offer an apology that you didn't owe me."

"Well, no," she admitted, only a trifle reluctantly. "Actually, I came to say goodbye. I dropped in at the center, to warn Human Resources that I wouldn't be working my notice, and to say my farewells to the girls on shift. Of all the people who weren't on shift, you're the only one I'd have regretted not saying goodbye to, so I sneaked a look at the records in HR and came over. You'll never see me gain—I hope that thought doesn't actually fill you with glee."

That was beyond amazing. The intensity of the shock informed me of how numb I'd become of late.

"You've got another job?" I said.

"No—I'm getting married."

She was watching me, looking for the reaction to that bombshell. I don't think I disappointed her. A full ten seconds must have passed before I managed to say: "Congratulations."

She grinned. "Congratulations yourself," she said. "You're the first person I've told not to look at me with horror and say: *You! Married!*"

"It is a trifle surprising, you have to admit. The idea of Trudi Hemming, the Empress Messalina of Leeds, falling in love…well, as you said yourself of the original Messalina, it doesn't quite fit in with your reputation."

"Who said anything about falling in love? I'm getting married. He's the one who's *in love*. It's not his first time—some blokes have an infinite capacity for self-delusion. His first wife walked away with a hundred thou, the second with five times that. He's reached the stage where his money makes more money of its own accord, although that certainly hasn't stopped him chasing even more. I reckon that I should get at least a million when he gets tired of me."

"Wow!" I said, lost in admiration, not so much for her cynicism as for the fact that she not only felt able to display it to me, but had actually made a special trip to do so. "Is that what you've been looking for all these years?"

"Of course not," she said. "I told you—I've been living in the moment. Sometimes, though, a moment comes along that offers you an opportunity. I'm grabbing it. Don't you think the old git will get value for his money?"

"Well…," I began.

"Don't say anything you'll regret," she said. "And before you mention Messalina again, I can do fidelity when it's politic. I've had enough pricks inside me to know that they're all pretty much the same, and that there's no point chasing after another if you have a sound reason for sticking with the one you've got."

It was obvious that she was challenging me; she actually wanted an argument. Maybe she wanted me to reassure her that she was doing the right thing, and maybe she wanted me to tell her that she was doing the wrong thing, although it wouldn't make any difference to what she did—but she did want an argument. She wanted to test herself. I felt quite proud to think that she'd chosen me to test herself against—although, in all honesty, there wasn't a lot of competition at the center.

"Actually, that surprises me," I said. "I haven't been in nearly as many cunts as you've allegedly had pricks inside you, but they were all different and distinctive."

"Yes, but I'm talking about men and you're taking about women. Women have personalities, physically as well as mentally, and they're versatile too—when you get bored sticking it in someone's cunt you can always stick it in her mouth or up her arse. Pricks, on the other hand, are just pricks, wherever they get stuck. And men, without exception, are just pricks."

Her eyes challenged me to deny it. I didn't. It wasn't a level playing-field, and I couldn't have won any kind of contest there. "So you're going to be a trophy wife?" I said.

"Is there any other kind?" Again, her eyes challenged me.

Again I ducked. "I suppose not," I agreed. "Marriage is, I suppose, essentially a matter of trophy-hunting, on both sides."

"God," she said, "You really are short in the ball department, aren't you? Aren't you even going to make an attempt to defend the true love that you and Sheena supposedly had? The *something more* that made you hesitate when I asked you whether you wanted to fuck me?"

"What would be the point? What proof could I possibly offer you that Sheena and I had something different? And what difference would it make to you if I did?"

"Take your shirt off," she said.

That was completely unexpected, and knocked me for six. I probably went pale.

"What?"

"You asked me what proof you could possibly offer me. Take your shirt off."

I couldn't believe that Sheena had ever shown Trudi her scars—but I could believe that Libby had told her good friend Tru about them, and had probably added speculations about their significance—only speculations, because I knew that Libby didn't know the truth.

"No," I said, bluntly; and added, in lower tone: "What difference could it possibly make?"

She shrugged. "None, I guess. I was just curious. I still think you're just a prick, mind—but Sheena was different. If Sheena had told me she loved you, I'd have believed her. And she didn't have to tell me, because I knew. And it's a crying shame that she's dead."

She didn't actually have tears in her eyes, but I thought that we had finally reached the real reason why Trudi didn't want to leave Leeds to be a trophy wife without first saying goodbye to me. She hadn't expressed her condolences at the funeral, or since, because condolences weren't her style—but she did have feelings, even though she was normally careful to keep them hidden.

"It is," I agreed, "And I'm sure, if Sheena were here, that she'd want to thank you for everything you did to help bring us together, as I do. She'd want to thank you for looking out for her, as I do. And she'd want to wish you good luck in your future life, as I do. She *is* still here, you know, in spirit, so you have, in fact, said goodbye to her."

"Luck," she said, quietly, "has nothing to do with it. For me, it's all strategy. For you, it was luck—the best you'll ever have—but you know that, don't you?"

"I do."

"And I'm not Messalina, no matter what you think. I'm Cleopatra—except that I'm marrying Julius Caesar, not Mark Antony, and I've no intention of offering my tit to an asp."

Her Classical education had obviously been coming along by leaps and bonds, but I leapt at the chance to correct the misconception.

"The myth about the asp is just a historian's lie," I said. "Cleopatra was murdered by Roman soldiers; the suicide story was invented fifty years after she was dead, to romanticize her. Some historians slander, others titillate—but they all lie."

"Irrelevant," she said. "As I said, I'm not doing that. I'm marrying Caesar, and when he gets tired of me, I'll walk away with a useful wedge of his assets. I don't need a Mark Antony, let alone a snake."

"Well, I hope you won't be offended if I say that I hope it works out for you, and that you fulfill all your dreams."

She looked at me intently. "You really do, don't you?" she said wonderingly.

"Why wouldn't I?" I said. "We're friends, aren't we?"

For two days, the fact that Trudi had quit work to run away with an aged millionaire who had fallen for her hook, line and sinker after a single night of passion—that bit was probably exaggerated—was the sole topic of gossip at the call center. Everybody marveled; all the girls expressed their envy—in Sheena's absence, there wasn't a single one who would even have thought of suggesting that there were more things in heaven and earth than were dreamt of in Trudi's philosophy.

Lily heard about it too, but to my great relief and delight, she didn't express envy, although she wasn't as censorious as she might have been.

"I wouldn't want to do it myself," she said. "It's just whoring. But I suppose she's still young. If she walks away with a big divorce settlement, she'll be able to marry for love the next time."

"Trudi doesn't believe in love," I told her. "That's the one thing she'll never do."

I said the same to Jez when he made the same observation, but he just nodded his head in agreement; he didn't meditate upon it the way that Lily had seemed to do.

After three days, everybody stopped talking about it—but Trudi wasn't forgotten the way some dropped topics were. She was a legend, and couldn't be put away. At girls' nights out, for years thereafter—at least, I assume so—there would always come a point in the general drunkenness when someone would reminisce about Trudi, and what a character she had been.

I was right, of course. I never saw Trudi again after that farewell visit, although she kept in touch with Libby Howell, and news has filtered back to Leeds through all these years.

I soon got a job in retail management with a supermarket chain, which didn't take long to post me down south, where I eventually ended up in Bournemouth, thus entitling me to say that I really do own property in Dorset now, albeit only a flat not much bigger than the one in Harehills Lane. Although I'm two hundred miles away, even when I'm not in Atlantis, I keep in regular touch with Lily, and visit her and Mum occasionally; the degrees of separation in their part of the city are still short enough to allow news to travel, especially where legends are concerned.

That's how I know that Trudi has negotiated her third divorce now, each one claiming a bigger slice of some aged prick's assets than the last. She lives in the south of France these days, on the Riviera, but she has a pied-à-terre in London, where Libby meets up with her occasionally for a girls' night out. I've never been invited, unsurprisingly, given that they hang out in places where a supermarket manager from Bournemouth definitely wouldn't fit in.

Is she happy? Who can tell? If she isn't, she'll never admit it.

Is anyone happy? Who can tell? At least I have no reason to think that any of the people who figured in that crucial phase of my life story is more than usually unhappy.

When Steve got out of the army, after failing to sustain any substantial wounds during his tours of duty in Iraq and Afghanistan, he got a job fitting and servicing alarm systems for industrial premises. He travels all over the north of England, and has a nice semi-detached house in Headingley, for which the sale of the Harehills Lane flat helped provide a deposit. He's married, with two children, both boys.

Lily is the intellectual star of the family; she's still in Leeds, working as a clinical psychologist. She married a fireman, and although it ended in divorce, she has a child, a little girl, that she loves very dearly, and she has a boyfriend who's an anesthetist, so I haven't given up hope for her by any means. I don't talk to her about it, of course, because if I were ever to break our mutually-agreed taboo against talking about intimate matters she'd reciprocate explosively, under the impulse of two decades of pent-up curiosity, academic psychology and dry shoulders.

Libby Howell is in retail management, like me, but in clothing—she'd probably say fashion, and it certainly seems to be close enough to allow her to tart herself up appropriately for her occasional binges with

Trudi. She's now married for the second time, with three kids; I forget what sex they are.

Jez got a job as a cameraman for local TV, and worked his way up to director before transferring down to London. He's divorced from someone he met at work—his real work, not the call center—with a son, although his ex-wife has custody. Rachel and Maxine are both married too, and both have kids, but I'm not sure how many.

I have no idea whether any of the above married for love, convention or security, or a mixture of the three—except in Lily's case, where it was most definitely for love, albeit love that turned out to have a short sell-by date.

Mum is increasingly forgetful, but still compos mentis. Even though she shows no real sign of senile dementia, I asked her once, when visiting, what were the things that stuck in her memory from long ago, and now seemed most precious. She said that it was the expression on our faces when the three of us were very small, when we saw her again after a brief period of absence, after nursery, or whatever.

"Your faces used to light up spontaneously," she said. "Only little children can do that."

I know what she meant. It doesn't take children long to lose that spontaneity of expression, to begin to guard their feelings, to be wary of showing their true feelings to the world. And I understood, too, why it meant so much to Mum to be able to remember that, because the idea that another human being can be spontaneously delighted simply by the sight of you after a brief absence...well, what can there possibly be in the vaults of memory that's more precious than that?

It's not just parents who have that brief privilege, although they probably have it more reliably. Lovers can have it too, albeit even more fugitively, and often with the lurking sensation that it might only be mimicry, not quite as spontaneous as it seems.

As for me, I'm still on the journey. I know where I'm headed, and even though I'm not at all certain that I'll get there soon, or ever, I haven't give up. I worry about it sometimes, especially when I remember that remark about diseased dreams that Sheena threw at me that time in the Merrion Centre. She certainly didn't think of her own dreams as products of disease—quite the opposite, in fact. She was ill, and knew it, after a fashion, but she always knew, too, that her dreams came from somewhere far beyond the reach of any kind of illness, and that they were utterly pure and spontaneous. Those are the kind of dreams I'm trying to grasp, but they're essentially elusive.

Some people might doubt the purity of Sheena's dreams, and my relationship with Sheena, but I don't. I can't. Sheena and I are bound by blood in a way that has nothing to do with clotting factors or defective genes: bound by the blood of the holy grail. If we weren't bound that way, she wouldn't be able to visit me occasionally, from a lot further away from the south of France, let alone Leeds, and we wouldn't still be together, albeit fitfully.

Sheena died a long time ago, as I said at the beginning of the story, but she changed me permanently, as vampires do, and there would be no way back even if I wanted one, which I don't, even though I haven't got to where I'm supposed to be going yet and our relationship is still incomplete. Perhaps it's only a matter of feeding the Muse, until she forgives me for the time it's taking for me to find her music and see her for what she really is—and to understand what I really am, even if I'll never be able to see it in a mirror.

Perhaps I'm simply incapable of remembering enough of the remote past ever find an identity capable of freeing Morgina, if any such identity ever existed, but I still hope that, as long as I have Sheena's help, there's a possibility that I—that we—might get there in the end.

The inhabitants of other times saw more colors in light than we can see, and they heard more harmony in music than we can hear. There's not much we can do to compensate for that, but we should do what we can. We can, at least, try our utmost not to think the way other people think, not to do the things other people do, not to like the things that other people like and not to want the things that other people want. We can feed the creatures of the night, and hope that one of those who accept our offerings will eventually set us free, in one or another of the nine or more secret ways that only Muses know.

In the meantime, if you can, live in love.

That's me, all over. *Carpe diem*, as Mark Antony would probably have said, if he had ever had to explain Cleopatra to his friends and countrymen, the Romans. Seize the day—and hang on to it, for dear life and beyond.

Never let it get away.